ON A ROLL

ALSO BY MELANIE GREENE

Roll of the Dice Series

Rocket Man *(Serena & Dillon)*

Ready to Roll *(Janice & Miguel)*

Eye of the Tiger *(Natalie & Evan)*

Let the Good Times Roll *(Chloe & Gabriel)*

Roll of a Lifetime *(Rachel & Theo)*

Roll Play *(Kim-ly & Tómas)*

On a Roll *(Gillian & Vic)*

Other Contemporary Romances

Retreat to Love *(Ashlyn & Caleb)*

Feather in Her Cap *(Jeannie & Brendan)*

Twelve Scorching Days *(Sarita & Scorch)*

ON A ROLL

MELANIE GREENE

For information, contact Melanie Greene at mel@melaniegreene.com

First edition: January 2021

On a Roll/by Melanie Greene

Cover Design by The Killion Group

Roll of the Dice Illustration by Alice Johnston

All rights reserved - used with permission

ISBN: 978-1-941967-22-5

To everyone fighting for a future that won't fight them back

CHAPTER ONE

WRAPPED IN A COZY ROBE, aromatic pillow warming her aching shoulders. Gentle music filling any silent space between the chatter of her lifelong best friends. Crackling fire in the marble fireplace. Hair-of-the-dog cocktail in hand.

Gillian heaved a huge sigh. She did not have time for all this.

"I know, right?" said Serena, a.k.a. the reason they were all trapped in a spa for the next several hours. "I'm in heaven."

Gill did not say a single sarcastic thing. It was a challenge to her stressed, overhung brain, but she met it. Instead, she settled deeper into her cushy lounger and took another sip of her peach Bellini, listening as Natalie read more service options off the spa's menu. Like they hadn't been over and over them, hadn't booked their whole day back before Gill's Thanksgiving break. She pasted a contented smile on her face and closed her eyes. Let everyone assume she was blissed out while they debated lunch. Her racing mind went straight back to grappling with the feedback to her teaching review.

"Everyone say hot stone massage." Natalie's bossiest voice indicated it was selfie time. Gill kept her eyes serenely closed, hoisting her glass while showing her teeth.

"Best bachelorette ever," Serena said, entirely against Nat's orders. But she was the bride; she could do as she liked.

Gill held her pose.

"Beautiful, great," someone said. Not Serena, not Natalie, not Rachel. A male someone. "How about now everyone stands in close to your pregnant friend?"

She dropped down her drink and opened her eyes. She was looking directly into a lens. Big, professional camera lens. Strong, firm fingers adjusting it, somehow both restless and sure of their movements. Behind the lens, a shaved head.

The others were laughing now, talking about the expression on her face—how it was priceless, how they hoped the photographer captured it. Personally, she didn't care one way or another if he had, so long as he wasn't ....

He was. "Hey, Gillian. Long time."

Amid her friends gasps of mirth, they peppered her with more questions. *You know him? Wait, you didn't tell me. And how precisely are you two acquainted?*

Bunch of nonsense, and she opted not to answer.

"Vic. Hi."

He wasn't quite bald, now she was examining him while trying to avoid meeting his eyes. A furze of grey-brown hair sprouted over his shapely head. Barely there, but still one of the significant ways his appearance had changed the past decade. Same intent, wiry frame. Same wide, lush lips. Same open, guileless gaze.

Not the same sex appeal. No. He'd managed to up that by a factor of a thousand or so. And from the glint as he took in how speechless he'd rendered her, he damn well knew it. The jerk.

"So, everyone, this is Victor Anthony. He's a friend of our pal Jorge, who used to work with me and Dillon? Took the photos at Jorge and Bubba's wedding, which is like the best rec possible, so of course I booked him for us. He's going to get a few shots of us this afternoon." Serena looked positively smug as she introduced Vic to Natalie and Rachel.

He shook their hands before turning to her. "And I've met Gilly-Bean."

Met. Tormented. She was a linguist, she ought to be able to come up with something more original than 'tomato ta-mah-toe' to express her ire. But that was Vic all over—such a persistent pest she couldn't come up with a coherent put-down.

Maybe it was the hangover. Or she was hyper-focused on her tenure committee deadline. Or all the lavender and eucalyptus in the neck pillow tricked her into relaxing the sarcastic part of her thought processes. "He's a friend of Anton's." Vic Anthony and Anton Bellamy—they'd been dubbed the Tony Twins back in elementary school, and never bothered to stop being best pals despite how growing up turned them into such different people. Her baby brother the mechanical engineer who spent half his time in Houston on lucrative contract jobs, the other half globe-trotting doing all that good works stuff that meant every twelfth journalist in the Northern Hemisphere had his contact info. And Victor, who starred in most of the school plays and took all the cast photos, who was always joining then quitting clubs and bouncing between social groups. Everyone loved Vic, but Anton was his only evergreen friend. The one at his side whether they were surrounded by the recycling committee or the improv players or the track team.

Three years, three months, three days. That's how much older she was than Vic. Anton had calculated that back when he and Vic were almost nine, and she'd told him that since she was three and a half years older than them, they had to stop whining that it was unfair if she got to stay up later than them. God, all those sleepovers, all those times he tagged along on camping trips or when they schlepped to the pool, all the CDs he snuck out of her room trying to convince Anton to care one whit about music, all the nights she had to sit in the carpool line outside the school waiting for them to be released from rehearsal. Starting in middle school, Anton did tech for every play Vic was in, and their parents volunteered her to do pickup as soon as she got her license. Back then, those years and months—but, okay, not the days—added up to a pretty big gulf between them. She spent way too much of her senior year dealing with her little freshman brother and his overactive freshman best friend, but then she was off to college while they, she assumed, found other people to pester. She managed to not see much of Vic when she made it home, other than being dragged to a couple of his plays because Anton just assumed she'd be up for it.

But then, Vic and Anton grew up. Mostly Vic. Anton never changed, studious and clever and inward-facing kid to studious and clever and inward-facing college student. And all these years later, studious and clever and inward-facing man, though she'd admit her brother looked like an actual adult now and not like a perpetually gawky boy.

Vic stopped looking like a kid when he shaved his prematurely grey hair as he emerged from high school. Or maybe it wasn't the lack of a boyish fringe flopping over his eyes. Maybe it was the way he settled into a stillness he'd never achieved around their dinner table all those years. Or how he stepped extra inches into her personal space over their chitchat during that first college spring break of his.

Whatever it was, those three years and three months and three days hadn't been much of a divide. Neither had his being her brother's best friend. Or their clothes. Their clothes hadn't proved to be any kind of barrier at all, in the end.

They'd run across each other in the decade since their one hot naked night. Of course they had; the Tony Twins were ride or die for each other. They'd never talked about it, though. Never repeated it.

Never been together in a room without Anton.

"Gilly-Bean?" Rachel giggled, which annoyed her. Rachel never used to giggle, not even back when they were all in college. Only around her daughter, but that was inevitable. Little Hannah could make anyone with half a heart giggle. Gillian decided to be dignified and blame this giggle on the pregnancy.

After all, the new baby would probably make them all giggle, too, once they got to meet her.

"It's one of Anton's annoying names for me. Though come to think of it, he never had annoying names for me before he met Vic." She glanced back at the man in question, and he was biting his lip like the most guilty of perpetrators.

He shrugged. "So how about that shot? Everyone around Rachel?"

The others just hopped to it, not in the least bothered by Vic's bossing them around or his clear glee at her discomfiture or his way of looking at her robe-clad self like he was aware of all her nakedness under the terrycloth.

She smoothed down the satin lapels as she rose from her lounge chair, making sure nothing he'd seen before would slip out. He crouched in front of them, acting all oblivious. Like he couldn't sense her rapid heart rate, the moisture flooding her mouth, the tingling heat at her core.

Well, he'd been a pretty slick actor back in school. No reason to think he'd lost the skill.

No reason to wonder which of his skills might, in the years since that one hot night, have gotten even better.

HE'D DRAWN UP SHORT, seeing her. Had to mess around with his equipment to cover for shaky hands. He wouldn't say trembling. That would be a shudder too far—it was more of a mild spasm, easily controlled as he followed the familiar routine of switching out lenses.

Besides, she didn't notice, blissed out sprawl of stillness that she was. Lost in thought again, for all that she was chipping in to the chatter of her girlfriends. Like that was a surprise. Gillian's brain could multitask like no other.

Not like his. He ripped his eyes off her to pay attention to the bride-to-be, Jorge's friend. Serena.

Focus, Vic.

His muscle memory kicked in, giving him a chance to catch up with himself. He worked the job. By the time Gillian's eyes snapped open to register his presence—damn straight he captured her fleeting look of outrage and self-consciousness, not that he'd be so rude as to include it in the portfolio—he had every system under control. As long as 'under control' could also be defined as 'reverting to the snarky brattiness of youth.'

Gillian could correct him. She had all the definitions packed into that big brain of hers.

And all the curves tucked into that robe. He didn't need her help defining those. He could recall them perfectly well. That night, back in college, that was the only time he'd had his hands on her. His mouth. His everything. But it hadn't been even close to the first time he'd studied her body. Damn, no wonder he'd just reverted to the teen brat, calling her nicknames. Ever since he first noticed girls, and sex, and hormones—a whole world of wide-awake skin and the joyous shock of orgasm—he'd noticed Gillian.

Not like he was unaware of her existence before his puberty turned her into a paragon. Ton's sister, just another resident of the Bellamy house when he threw himself into it any time he could. Like Mr. and Mrs. B, Gillian was a quick 'hi' on their way to Anton's room, or someone to set a place for at dinnertime, or another person in the world who'd probably notice if a vortex opened up and sucked him into another dimension.

And then she passed him the bread basket one normal Wednesday night, and his skinny boy fingers brushed her purple-nailed hand, and ... things happened inside him. Things that made him glad for the neatly-ironed tablecloth and Mr. B's rambling story about some work crisis saving him from having to speak or meet anyone's gaze for a good while.

So, yeah, he knew Gill's curves, no matter how many robes she hid within.

Focus, Vic.

He dug deep to lasso the professional patter, kept his attention on the bride-to-be, ran through the groupings as they moved past the spa pools to their lunch table. It was almost like he was capable of fulfilling his contractural obligations even while he burned to corner Gillian and figure out what kind of chemistry they had when Anton wasn't on the scene.

CHAPTER TWO

THE TEXT THREAD from the gals was going to push her over the edge. She had to keep up with it. No option, not three days before Serena's wedding. They'd all been friends since meeting at University of Texas a dozen years earlier. They'd settled into Houston one by one—her last of all, once her first post-doctorate placement and a smidgen of luck bounced her high enough up the ladder of academia to land her an assistant professorship.

No matter what forces pulled at her as she was yoked to the publish-or-perish realities of her career, her gals abided. They listened to rants about interdepartmental feuds, toasted the beginning and end of each teaching term, prodded her for stories about the latest nonsensical student questions. They were her support system.

And she was part of theirs. All three of her BFFs were getting married over the next several months—Serena to Dillon on New Year's Day, Natalie to Evan on their shared birthday in April, and Rachel to Theo in early summer, a few months after their baby's expected birth. Maybe by the time the last one rolled around, everyone would be so over wedding rigamarole they'd just saunter to the courthouse and thence to Theo's pub for beer and cake. But with two days until the New Year's Eve rehearsal dinner, and seemingly limitless pages of undone to-do lists, the gals were all hands on deck, all thumbs to keyboards. The text chains spooled out fast and urgent.

Which was fine. Serena wasn't overboard with her worries so much as way fonder of lists than someone as artsy as she ought to be, stereotypically speaking. Her shared Google sheets featured precise, color-coded, time-lined tasks. The other brides-to-be had already copied them as templates for their own nuptials. Gill was excited to see it all coming together, thrilled for her friends, eager to help.

If only they'd leave Vic out of it.

She'd escaped to a treatment room as he was wrapping up his shoot at the day spa. He'd laughed. Out loud. At her. And said, "Running won't help you for long, Dill Pickles. I've got hours left of this gig, and Anton's bound to give me your number if I ask."

Serena, a traitor to the core, made sure to sing out, "I'll give you her number, Vic." And then they'd laughed. Together. Out loud. Took a good few minutes of piped-in white noise and the ministrations of a professional to smooth the sounds from her mind.

Either she hadn't followed through on the threat, or Vic wasn't bothered about talking to her after all. The twelve million —like most people, she gravitated toward a set number when speaking hyperbolically—texts per hour were all from Serena, Natalie, and Rachel. They pried and intruded and dug for more about Vic, no matter how much she ignored those questions and concentrated on the important stuff. Like when she could pick up the dessert for the rehearsal dinner. And if Frijoles' manager had the final head count for their New Year's Eve countdown.

It didn't stop them from interrupting an in-depth conversation about the babysitter Theo had lined up to watch his and Rachel's children to detail the exact times that Vic would be at the venue, or for Serena to add 'proofread the photographer's list of essential shots for the ceremony' to Gillian's to-do list.

Subtle.

Ignoring her friends' agenda, Gillian focused on the important stuff. She texted Natalie to meet her at the gym, knowing Nat needed a few minutes to vent about Serena's dad, Duncan. For a year or so when they were kids, Serena's dad and Natalie's mom were married, until he left her for a teacher at Natalie's synagogue. Nat had volunteered to wrangle the man throughout the wedding events, which left her answering his grumbling about been relegated to the role of usher, along with his teenage son from his third or fourth marriage. Serena and Dillon had decided to walk each other down the aisle, and both of her parents were put out about it.

"Well, at least he's predictable."

"I suppose that's something," Natalie agreed. "I can't believe that man used to be my ideal father figure."

"I am pretty sure you've changed your mind about any number of things since you were twelve."

"Not an age with tons of nuance," Nat agreed.

"To understate the matter."

"So, speaking of understatements, that photographer seems a little tiny bit interested in you."

Here she was doing the woman a service, giving her space to complain so she could treat Duncan with equanimity and not add to Serena's stress. Look what it got her: more interrogation. She amped up the speed on her elliptical, like that would somehow help her run away from this conversation. "Nat."

"Hey, if you don't want to talk about it, just say so."

"I don't want to talk about it."

"No problem. After all, we've been friends for so long now. We know each other's limits, when to let something drop."

"Uh-huh." Her tone made clear she wasn't in the least fooled by the Nat's cheerful acceptance.

"All those years. Sometimes I can't believe how much we've gone through together. And I don't just mean the group project for Professor Scarano's microbiology class."

"You swore you'd never mention industrial fermentation to me ever again."

"Did I mention it? By name, I mean? Don't worry," Nat said. "I have an excellent memory for our college days, but that doesn't mean I go around naming every incident."

"Hey, I'm not the one who crashed the university's golf cart into the bushes."

"It was my job!"

Gillian grinned. "Driving the cart was your job, not crashing it."

"It wasn't damaged. Anyway, like I said, I'm not the one going around naming incidents. Like, you won't catch me saying, 'Remember that time you came back from spring break senior year and swore me to secrecy and told me you'd hooked up with your brother's best friend and it was the best sex of your life?'"

Oh, fuck. She'd blocked out how she totally spilled every bean about Vic. "Damn you and your memory."

"Yep. Thought you'd reply something like that—if I was the kind of person to go around naming incidents from our past. That's why I'm such a good friend and would never mention it."

She was so screwed. "Don't tell the others."

Natalie rolled her eyes. "Duh."

"And it's not like I haven't seen him since then. He's still Anton's best friend."

"But I gather you've both kept your clothes on around each other since then?"

"Obviously."

"How come?"

"What do you mean?" Gill knew what she meant. She was stalling.

"How come," Natalie repeated, "you're letting all that sizzle between you and Vic fizzle into nothing? It's not like you to ignore something like that."

Gillian eyed the elliptical's control panel. If she upped the resistance, her friend might just buy that she was too winded for conversation.

"Hey."

Or not. She sighed. "Okay. Fine. Look, you know how Anton is. Even with all the work he's put into it, he struggles with social skills. He doesn't have all that many friends, and he said once that with most of them, he spends so much time second-guessing himself and trying to read their reactions that he can't just ... relax and enjoy. You know? But he's not like that with Vic. They've never had any trouble being around each other. Vic doesn't criticize him or get tired of him or take him aside and ask him to 'please just act normal' because he wants to introduce him to someone new."

"Some fucker said that to Anton?"

"Yeah, more than one someone. I've heard it myself. One guy tried to enlist me to help, asked how I explained my brother to others. In front of him."

"What a shithead."

"The grimiest of putrescent snotweasels. I shut him down. Obviously."

"I hope he still flinches when he thinks about it."

She blew out a measured breath, because there was running away from Nat's interrogation, and then there was letting her big sister wrath slam-kick her heart rate into dangerous territory. "Oh, I feel sure he does."

Natalie let the silence settle around them a while. Or, if not silence, the usual gym soundscape of machines and chatter and upbeat hits from the last century. Nat wasn't letting anything drop, though. "So you're protective of their friendship. I get that."

"Thanks." She meant it. Hearing Natalie articulate and vali-date her fears helped her feel less like she was blowing things way out of proportion.

"Sure. It's not like we haven't all been the beneficiary of your mama bear tendencies before. You're like our gallant knight, always ready to charge into battle and knock heads."

Was she? Okay. Interesting. Note to self: take a kickboxing class. Not that she could imagine engaging in actual physical altercations, but she was oddly warmed by her friend's assessment. "Well, if I am, maybe that generated from me playing the protective sibling. Just—here I go trying not to explain my brother again—I think plenty of older siblings look out for the younger ones. It's nothing to do with Anton specifically."

Nat shrugged as much as she was able given their treks to nowhere on the machines. "Only child here; what do I know?"

"Well, I'd say ask Evan, but I'm sure that would lead to him grumbling a little." Natalie's fiancé was the youngest of five. He'd had his fill of siblings sticking him in their boxes and treating him like he wasn't up to independent adulthood.

"I know we're all about Serena's wedding right now, but have I mentioned how many nieces and nephews that man has? Duncan's grousing about having to usher with Jonas, but at least Serena and Dillon managed to find official jobs for all of their relatives. We haven't got a clue how to assign tasks without offending someone."

"Draw names from a hat?"

"We may have to. The whole Lee family group chat is all about dropping hints these days."

Gill narrowed her eyes at Nat. "So you know what it's like."

"What what's like?"

Gill dead-panned at her.

"Oh, right, the focus on your photographer."

"Ha. Ha. Ha."

"Sorry, that was pathetic. I'll make better puns next time."

"Or you could stop making puns at all."

"You've met my fiancé. It turns into an unbreakable habit."

"Bet you could break it if you tried. Try not mentioning Vic at all, that'll help."

"And what's going to stop the others? Do you want me to intervene?"

"No, but thanks. I don't feel much like a gallant knight if I can't even wage my own war."

They moved on to other topics, and Gillian told herself that getting the gals to stop mentioning Vic every few hours was all she really wanted. Her twelve millions fleeting thoughts about him maybe contacting her independent of the wedding work didn't matter in the least.

CHAPTER THREE

HE TUCKED the printout of Gillian's excessively detailed and detached email into his breast pocket and headed into Frijoles, the Tex-Mex place where Serena and Dillon's rehearsal dinner would be shortly underway. After introducing himself to the manager on duty, he headed to the party room to get a few establishing shots of the layout and the tres leches parfaits and the lines of margarita glasses stretched along the bar.

Gillian, he figured, would come in with the rest, after they'd done the actual rehearsal. The bride and groom had opted to skip his services at the chapel in favor of him sticking at the party later. Their mutual friend Jorge would act as his assistant for an hour of secondary shots, once the speeches were underway, but this party was fairly laid back and intimate. He found himself in the not-quite-friend not-just-professional zone with these two, not for the first time. He'd known them from a few parties at Jorge and Bubba's before the wedding, and he'd helped Serena out with some photos for work a couple of times.

In the past, with friends-of-friends, or overly effusive wedding couples, he'd taken care to draw firm lines. He was a vendor, with a job to do. That came first no matter how much he liked the subjects of his work. But his job was an intimate one, capturing not just the pretty dresses and elegant guests, but, when he was both skilled and fortunate, raw emotion.

For that, he needed a layer of reserve, of distance between himself and his subjects. That's what the lenses were for: a handy outward manifestation of the way he was eternally the one on the outside. The observer.

So when a groom slung an arm over his shoulder and invited him to down a shot, or a flirty attendant suggested he drop the camera and dance, he pled professional duties. The life of a friendship, after all, was longer than one wedding season. If he was meant to have a personal relationship with a client, they could build it after the shots were delivered and the invoice paid.

That said, this event was on a countdown to midnight. And no matter how he fussed with his equipment or checked off tasks, he was constantly aware of the passing time. When midnight hit, he'd take a pic of the engaged couple celebrating the new year, but then ... then he planned to be kissing Gillian Bellamy.

EVERYONE COULD SEE she was super busy. It was the night before one of her very most important person's wedding. There'd been the copious nonsense at the rehearsal with Serena's dad and mom and stepdad, when she'd found herself front and center for the drama. Forced into jumping up and down waving her arms to distract them all. Then the manager at Frijoles cornering her with questions, and then those guests besieging her to gush about how cute the kids had been. She didn't know if they thought she was Dillon's sister, or Rachel, or not a parent at all but just a fellow admirer of little Tobias and Hannah, but the point was: she was super busy.

So she had zero spare time for his pointed looks. His circling the room not like it was his job, but like he was a gyroscope and she was the epicenter. She talked to the lead bartender about midnight champagne; Vic was posing Dillon and Serena on a pair of Frijoles' colorful bar stools. She checked in with Natalie to make sure all the step-siblings were playing sweet; Victor Anthony was right behind her suggesting that throwing fake gang signs was best left to group prom photos instead of the wedding party of fully grown mostly white people. She couldn't move five feet without being aware of his gaze.

"What's got you glum?" Rachel asked.

"Nothing ."

"Oh for sure, a fake chirpy voice and that crocodile smile has me convinced you've never partied so hard," her friend said. Which was the flip side of having shared an apartment with someone for years; no matter how long ago it'd been. She wasn't the least adept at being unreadable to Rach.

"It's nothing. Just Vic."

"He ducking up the job?"

"Ducking?"

"Six-year-old and three-year-old at home. I thought I had more time to learn to watch my language, but then I went and fell for a guy with a school-aged son."

Gill laughed. "Ducking it is then."

"So he is ducking it up? You need me to go quack at him?"

She wrapped an arm around Rach and turned them so they were facing the entrance to the party room. "No quacking necessary. It's only that he ... it feels like maybe he ...."

Wow. The linguist unwilling to articulate something.

"Is it the way he hasn't taken his eye off you for more than three minutes at a time even though he's supposed to be busy capturing the precious final minutes of Serena and Dillon as single people?"

Gill snatched up an abandoned cloth napkin and thwapped it against the table for emphasis. "Yes. It is exactly that. He won't stop looking at me."

And then Rachel was leaning against her so hard Gill

panicked in case it was pregnancy distress. But despite the haze
of adrenaline shooting through her she gathered quickly that
Rach was fine. Doubled over laughing at her, which ought to be
grounds for a serious girlfriend talking-to, but fine.

"What?"

"You—you are so ...."

"So what? Stop giggling. Everyone's looking at us."

"Everyone? Or mostly just one person in particular?"

"Shut it, you." Not that there was any heat in her words. Not
that anyone really noticed them. Not that she was keeping
herself from peering over Rachel's bent form at Vic.

He winked at her.

Jerk.

She so did not need this kind of attention. She could imagine
her parents' narrowed eyes at the very idea that she was being
overdramatic and attention-seeking with her personal life. At
work, okay, she was encouraged to feel pride when her students
were attentive to her lessons. To the material. To the ways their
studies interacted with her field.

But attention paid to her as a person, outside of the scope of
educator and researcher and writer? No. It made her self-
centered to fuss over friend dynamics, and the need to protect
her perfectly competent and successful baby brother, and a heart
that—damn it to perdition and rake it with the ashes of hellfire
—seemed to give a through, thumping damn about exactly the
kind of attention Vic was paying it.

Theo wandered over to check on Rachel, which was just the
distraction Gillian needed to refocus on what was important.
Not her weird heart longings, but the successful gathering of
Serena and Dillon's friends and families. Surely one of Serena's
parents was doing something stress-inducing somewhere. It was
Gill's duty to shield everyone from their shenanigans.

And never mind the man whose job it was to capture
everyone without their shields. To see into their hearts and make

permanent images of what Gillian—what anyone—might prefer to leave hidden away.

———————

SHE THOUGHT she was so good at hiding.

Ha.

Maybe it would work on someone who hadn't known her since they were in elementary school, but not on him. He knew her tells. Hadn't he listened to her fudging truths at the family dinner table, while he had the inside scoop? Hadn't he been there when Ton told her that she could drop the protective-big-sis stance, because of course Vic knew about his best friend's sexual orientation?

Hadn't he lived through every excruciating second of that first pool party after they'd slept together in college? Gillian as blasé as always, no one else catching that minuscule moment when they'd locked eyes. How she'd buried her thoughts almost —almost—sooner than he could see the intense flare of longing. She'd banked it so fast, but: he knew her tells. Her unspoken message to stay away, that they weren't happening ever again, had been clear. She didn't hide it at all. But so was the quieter message that she was warning off herself as much as she was him.

So let her bob and weave her way through the rehearsal dinner party. No problem for him. It wasn't midnight quite yet, and he had a job to do.

Ten minutes to countdown, and he was posing all the brides-maids with their noisemakers and streamers ready to go.

Eight minutes, and he caught the groom's sister and brother-in-law both reaching to smooth Dillon's hair while he batted them away, laughing.

Five minutes. An overhead shot of the room, of that moment when people caught the buzz of the approaching midnight, and started to seek out those they wanted close when the New Year rang in. Gillian drifting his way as he stood on a chair in the corner.

Three minutes to go, he closed in on the wedding party. They'd all clustered together, the bride's and groom's best friends and their partners, if they had them. Gillian wasn't the only one without a date in the excitable group hug that enclosed Serena and Dillon. Just the one who was closest to him.

One minute. One half-step to bring him beside her as she took charge of telling the room about countdown. Yes, he was focused on the people who were paying him. He was a professional, and he was damn good at his job.

So good he could capture Serena and Dillon locked on to each other, frozen in a moment of realization that midnight would mean the end of their last days as single people. The hint of tears in his eyes and the captivated grin on her face, lost to everyone buzzing around them.

Thirty seconds, and they laughed and laced their fingers together and looked around with wonder-filled gazes as the crowd they'd assembled to celebrate with them.

Ten seconds. Nine, eight, seven. Gillian ignoring him— pretending she was ignoring him—while she led the countdown chant. Four. Three. Two.

Explosions of cheers and song and confetti and bodies jostling. He was planted within it all, solid and sure taking shots of the midnight kisses. Every smiling face. Every glint and glitter.

And then he'd done it. And it was the New Year. And he lowered his lens, took that last half-step to bring them flush, and ran the back of his fingers down Gillian's cheek. Held her gaze. Read past her expected give-nothing-away look to the truth inside her.

Her breath hitched, and there was confetti glinting in her braids, and his heart pounded like the beat of the mariachis playing behind them. His feet were planted so the people jostling them didn't affect him. But maybe they did her, or maybe she opted to press herself closer and wrap her hands around his biceps, but it was a new year, and it was his same old feelings about his best friend's big sister, and she wasn't, just for that one transitional, magic moment, hiding from him.

So he kissed her.

CHAPTER FOUR

"Sooooooo ...."

Gillian glared at Rachel, daring her to keep the sing-song syllable going. Being trapped at side-by-side manicure stations didn't exactly give her any leverage, though.

Especially with Serena and Natalie joining in the cursed chorus of curiosity. "Couldn't help but notice you ringing in the New Year," Serena said. "But next thing you know, I look around and Vic is still taking pictures and I can't find you anywhere."

"You know I turn into a pumpkin at midnight."

"First off," Rachel said, "It's the coach that turns into the pumpkin, not Cinderella. And second, we roomed together for half a decade, and now you're trying to convince me you're not a night owl?"

"Barely three years."

"Regardless." Rachel's free hand flapped her way. "You definitely kissed Vic, and then you definitely were gone while the rest of us wrapped up the party, and he definitely was still there after you left. So. What's the story?"

"Ditto." Natalie and Serena looked at each other and grinned. Back when the four of them roomed together at college, they did that all the time—jumped in with 'ditto' when someone else asked for the latest gossip.

Gillian didn't bother rolling her eyes, since only the manicurist would get the full effect, but she did sigh loudly at her best friends. "Is this really the first time in y'all's thirty-odd years that you've heard of the tradition of kissing someone at midnight?"

"Oh, I didn't realize the way you clung to him like he was keeping you afloat in a raging sea was just you being *traditional*," Rachel said. The others snorted.

"Don't deconstruct the moment just cause I was the only one without a fiancé in tow. I'm allowed my good luck kiss without it having to carry some massive big meaning behind it." Even she could tell she was floundering, but she kept to her story. "Vic was the closest unattached person when midnight rolled around. It doesn't have to be momentous that we kissed for a hot second."

"That was not one solitary second," Natalie said.

"It was hot, though," added Rachel.

One hand with drying nails, one hand surrendered to the manicurist's attentions, no easy way to flip off her friends.

She shrugged, like they weren't becoming burrs wrapped tight into her bridesmaid coiffure. "It was just Vic. I've known him since he was, like, eight."

"Not eight anymore."

Gillian ignored the speculation in Nat's tone. "Twenty-eight. Still a baby. Plus, he's Anton's best friend. Number of nights he spent at our house, he's practically a second little brother to me."

What happened that once in college was not a bit fraternal, but the others didn't need to know that. Except Nat, who kept quiet. Besides, back then she'd finally gotten to accepting herself for who she was, instead of contorting herself into the pattern cut for her by her family. Once Anton—brave, amazing Anton— went and shattered his own mold, she'd figured out she could do the same. And part of that shattering was accepting her life wasn't wife-and-mother bound. Free of the expectations of husband hunting, she figured out what she wanted out of her dating life. Fun, some intellectual stimulation, and lots of sensual stimulation.

For a flash of time, she got all that with Vic. But he was one of several. No reason to dwell on it then, or mention it now.

Serena caught her eye. "Just saying, the man is pretty. And don't think any of us missed how he was watching you all night."

"Or how he looked at you at the spa," added Natalie.

"Or how you looked at his zoom lens." Rachel had come over all madonna-like, running marigold-tipped fingers over the swell of her abdomen, acting like she wasn't cracking up everyone in the room.

Even Gillian. So she stifled the speech she'd been contemplating, about how just because the three of them were set to marry over the next few months, they didn't need to go inventing a relationship for her.

Bad enough all these weddings meant being trapped in make-up chairs and having her hair yanked around into fancy shapes and wearing form-fitting dresses and offering up her feet for pumicing and her fingers for shellacking. She didn't need to compound the torment of beautification with the emotional and intellectual trial of rehashing all her reasons for staying single.

"BEAUTIFUL, perfect hold that. And a bit more of a squeeze in together. Okay. Everyone turn your heads to the right. Your other right. Now back at me and smile."

He blathered on with his congenial patter, calculated to get the whole wedding group on his side so they could get their shots done and move on to the partying.

Not that he allowed himself to operate on auto pilot during these formal pictures. It was a matter of experience, of skill. Every happy family and all that—he knew what they wanted. The relatives moved out and he clustered the bridesmaids around Serena. "Okay, and the bouquets across your right arms.

Rachel, are you okay to lean towards the left for me? Great, thanks. How about ...?"

He shifted a foot to the side. It wasn't the light, it was the dresses. He just needed ... he walked forward and found himself face-to-face with Gillian. "It's okay if I snag this?" He tugged one of the big orange daisies from her bouquet. She gave him a look but opted against the verbal tongue lashing he had a feeling was trapped behind her social smile.

She made it impossible for him to go away. To leave her alone. Probably she had all kinds of other opinions on what was and was not possible, but he knew what he knew. He snapped off most of the stem and tucked the daisy into her raven hair. Breathed past the tingle when his fingertips brushed her brow. Struggled to ignore her spice-sweet scent. Stepped back and considered the group. Nodded. "Perfect. Okay, Gilly-Bean, stop glaring and smile. Or laugh, like your friends." He snapped up her expression, not that it would go front and center on his website. The glower would scare potential clients. He had a feeling, though, that Serena would like it. She was clearly enjoying every moment of her wedding day, including his somewhat bratty treatment of Gillian.

Serena's sense of humor wasn't as snide as Gillian's, but he'd noted her fondness for gentle teasing. Pics of a disgruntled Gillian would suit her funny bone, though she wouldn't opt to display them. He'd keep that pleasure in reserve for himself.

He reigned himself in from thoughts of decorating his home gallery with portraits of Gillian. And of the two of them. And group shots of him flanked by Gill and Ton.

Lowering the lens, he winked at her. She was too busy basking in the moment with her friends to bother blistering him with any one of her many opinions. Bride and bridesmaids all had relaxed into comfortable body language, making it a breeze to capture all the ways their connection had them brimming with love for Serena.

"Okay, groomsmen and Dillon. Come join the fun." It all got

companionable after that. Once they'd moved en masse to the reception hall, he packed up some equipment for his assistant to stash in the SUV and switched up what he needed for the indoor work. And reset himself while he was at it. Never mind the press and taste of her midnight kiss lingering on his senses, never mind her radiating beauty captured for eternity with his camera. Those things weren't the job. And he knew enough about Gillian Linette Bellamy to understand that anything short of brilliance for her friend's wedding photos would drop him so far beneath her consideration he might as well not inhabit her same universe.

So he did the job. Last thing he wanted was to give Gill any excuse to disdain him. They'd lived through too many years of close encounters that kept her from seeing him as anything but Ton's pal and a tag-along nuisance for her family.

He had goals, and being considered a nuisance wasn't among them.

CHAPTER FIVE

RODEO SEASON WAS APPROACHING, so Anton showed up in Houston again. His agricultural engineering jobs kept him hopping all over the world, but he never booked anything to interfere with when the Houston Livestock Show and Rodeo needed him. It wasn't so much the agri-business or cowboy culture or even his love of fried turkey legs. It was that, unexpected though it was, the rodeo was the first place he'd felt free to be his truest self without enduring criticism. Once he started interning with HLSR he'd found people who didn't care about so many of the things that made him stick out in ways their family found aggravating. The social difficulties, the way he excelled only in the parts of school that mattered to him, his please-don't-mention-it-maybe-it's-a-phase sexual orientation.

She should let her brother know that his endurance of their folks' reaction when he came out to them had infused her with strength when she discovered—and announced—her bisexuality.

Anyhow, the rodeo people didn't just take him as-is. They celebrated him. It was where her baby brother learned he wasn't going to spend his entire life limited to two people who understood and accepted him. His sister and his best friend were great, he'd said, but he felt less like he had to cling to their approval when he knew his way of moving through the world could be an asset. Could be exactly what someone was looking for.

Vic had teased him, back in their final year of high school, about how watching the cowboys was a bigger deal than discovering a way to work that didn't shove Anton into a constraining mold.

"Nope," he'd said, tossing a balled up piece of paper Vic's way. "I'm too attractive to go forever without a boyfriend. And look at Gillian, she got even prettier once she left for college. Odds are I will, too."

She'd thrown her own paper ball at Anton, then. "Hey."

"You did, though, didn't you?" Her brother was oblivious about her discomfort. But it was, she supposed, just him and Vic, so whatever. She could tolerate talking about herself without fear they'd paste on that 'Gillian is looking for praise again' disapproval her parents expressed when she let out any hint of her needy vanity.

"You did." Vic glanced away as soon as she looked at him, rubbing at the greying hair covering his scalp.

Poor kid. He always rubbed at his head when he was self-conscious. She didn't think his teenager-with-grey-hair situation took away from his looks any, but compared to the objective beauty of Anton, maybe he was as prone to questioning his appearance as she was if she let her parents' opinions live in her head.

Maybe.

Anyway, he didn't need the reassurance of a big-sister type. Or so she'd guessed at the time. Not two years later, during her senior and his freshmen year college spring break, she found out Vic had a not-at-all-brotherly regard for her opinions. But before they got much time to explore what that meant, things went to shit with Anton, and that spiraled them away from each other in what was, she decided in all her twenty-one-year-old wisdom, for the best.

Ten years on, and she and Vic only skirted around each other when Anton was in town, and that was enough for her. It wasn't like the two of them often needed to co-exist away from Anton. So it didn't matter about Serena's wedding or the New Year's Eve kiss or anything else. Anton showed up in Houston, filling the other side of their duplex with noise and energy and whatever magnets he had that worked on her and Vic and a few other specific people, but no one else.

Anton said he didn't need anyone else; Gillian tried to believe him. Even at Rodeo time, when his eyes jumped restlessly past every person, and he ate sporadically enough to hollow out his cheeks, and the only times he was still were when Vic was in the room.

"Tony!"

"Tony." Anton stood back to let Vic in the house. Their hug went motionless when Vic noticed her sitting on the sofa.

"Hey," she said, like it was nothing to see him again.

Because it wasn't.

"Pickles."

Anton laughed, one of the laughs that shook his bones, so she didn't object. She just shifted over so the Tonys could join her, Anton squashed between her and Vic as if they were his own personal weighted blankets. Probably he'd measured their collective width when sofa shopping, just to be sure he could maintain this squeeze with them when he needed it.

"So what's happening?" She wasn't asking Vic, as he well knew, but that didn't stop him from answering.

"I'm meeting with your friends tomorrow to show them the proofs. Did they tell you?"

She shook her head.

"Oh, I forgot Vic did Serena's pics. Was it as color-coordinated and free-flowing as she could have wished?"

"Ha. Of course. She wasn't allowing any other option for her and Dillon's big day."

Anton's laugh for her was quieter, but deeper within him. She couldn't help the smile she exchanged with Vic. They both knew the pleasure of being someone Anton was happy to respond to.

Vic rattled on about work and about the neighbor across the street who used to terrify the boys when they were growing up—Vic bought out his parents when Mr. and Mrs. Anthony retired to sail the world—and about some mystery series they both liked.

She'd have crossed the porch to her half of the house, but Anton held both their hands and was letting her rest her head on his shoulder. Plus, he hadn't spilled about the real reason he was skittery-scattery, and Gill knew Vic's patter would help ease it out of him.

"Cisco doesn't like to read."

Vic didn't hesitate at the topic change. "Doesn't he, then?"

"Nope. Not saying he's not smart."

"Sure, course."

"Just that reading isn't his thing. Says I read enough for ten people so he'll take the time and use it for music and riding instead."

"He's a cowboy?" Gillian hoped she never blushed as bright as her brother. Blessed the darker shade of her skin.

"Francisco Martine, yeah. One of the best."

She felt Vic's nudge as it passed through to Anton's other shoulder. "And he's into music?"

"Yeah. Reminds me of you that way."

And that's why she wasn't kissing Vic again, no matter how many midnight countdowns they spent together. Not when her red-cheeked, antsy, picky-in-love brother still compared every man he fell for to his one and only best friend.

VIC KNEW the newlyweds loved color. Or Serena did, in a way that influenced Dillon, too. So he pulled out his mom's orange and yellow lap blankets and tossed them artfully over the client chairs. Hung some of his framed still life flower arrangements on the office wall. It wasn't pandering. He did it, when he had a sense of his customers, to make them more at ease. They wanted to be thrilled about his photos, but they also wanted to feel known enough to be comfortable critiquing the work.

Anyway, they were friends with Gillian. And with Jorge. Also, they worked with photos at their marketing firm. So he didn't expect them to be hesitant to call his stuff crap, if they felt it.

But it didn't hurt to make the space welcoming. And if they mentioned to Gillian how much they liked working with him, fine. He didn't need a professional endorsement to make points with her.

He'd admit to wanting to make points with her.

Not to her directly. Not even to Anton, who would think him sentimental and hung up on childish things. But to himself, Vic could admit it.

He'd even admit that his crush on her in high school was childish. It seemed pretty common, guys falling for friends of their sisters, or sisters of their friends. What girl did he know any better than the one he sat across from at dinner two or three times a week, and slept down the hall from practically every weekend? When he started to ID specifics about who he was attracted to, of course he narrowed the field from 'girls' to 'girls with dark hair' and 'girls who liked camping, even if it was just in the back yard cause her family didn't think it was safe for a girl to head into the woods for a weekend with her friends' and 'girls who made sarcastic comments as casually as possible so you had to think maybe they were being sincere at first but then you get a look at the tilt of their eyes and knew they were daring you to hold in your laugh.'

Made sense, was all. He'd had plenty of time since high school to both broaden and refine the list of people he was likely to fall for.

Gillian happened to still fit every kind of bill he could imagine, but that was his mature, adult take on things. Not the childishness of lingering at her parents' dining table to wait out an inconvenient erection cause her jeans were tight and she bent to clear the serving bowls. Not even the college memories of the two of them almost naked but never quite talking about how they were almost naked, pressed together, and then she was touching him, not everywhere he'd ever dreamed of but in crucial, urgent places, and she was letting him touch her the same way and then she told him where she kept her condoms and he made enough of an inquiry to be sure she was sure and she tasted like sunshine and long nights rolled into one and the exact degree of their nakedness didn't impede either of them and maybe that was just lust and sex and a lot of fantasies overlaid on the lust and knowing they could trust each other even while the lust kept their hands on each other, even while they tasted and undulated and it was dreams grown up into an explosion of rightness but they still, never quite, talked about it again.

Nope. None of that impacted the reasons he and Gill, ten years on, should be making points with each other.

And if giving her friends cozy throw blankets and brewing a fresh pot of coffee meant they might call him good to work with, that was just networking prowess on his part.

Gillian Linette Bellamy, no matter how well she wore her leggings at her brother's house the day before, had nothing to do with it.

CHAPTER SIX

"LET me help you with the wrangling, then I'll go help Nat."

"I've got the kids, it's fine." Serena shot her a look indicating that Gill was the one being antsy and overboard about the set-up for Rachel and Theo's party.

Couldn't be wronger. Gillian was cool like a mojito with extra mint. Theo's brewpub and restaurant, Elixir, was closed to the public for the night, and the friends converged in advance of everyone else to decorate and otherwise manage all the couple would need to celebrate their engagement. And their forthcoming baby. And Theo's name day on top of the rest.

She and Serena had hauled Rachel's daughter Hannah and Theo's son Andres to the Children's Museum for the afternoon, getting them plenty tired and a little too sugared up. Worth it. They'd cracked each other up at the rubber duck races and Andres showed off an unsuspected skill on the dance floor in the motion room. Now they needed to herd them into Elixir, but Natalie texted to ask for help with the balloons. Because what the party needed was balloons. It wasn't already a decor explosion with Theo's glittery name day banner and the baby-shaped confetti and a mass of pink and white bouquets scattered everywhere. Not to mention all the Valentine's Day decorations still covering Elixir's walls and windows.

May as well throw in a steamer trunk covered in bon voyage stickers and a few fireworks and perhaps a petting zoo.

Still, Serena seemed as under control as someone herding two excited little kiddos could be, so Gill went in search of Nat. She was parked around the side of the brewpub, and the sight of her crouching into the backseat of her SUV trying to get ahold of all the balloon ribbons wafting around her just about did Gill in.

"Didn't you tie them in bunches before you loaded them up?" She slid into the passenger seat and batted back some of the orange and green and blue floating orbs.

"Don't you be logical with me, Gillian Bellamy. I am not in the mood."

"Or maybe you should have brought the helium tank here and filled them on site?"

"The mood. Not in it."

She snagged a handful of ribbons and started to wrap them into a knot. Nat copied her, until they had all the balloons corralled in bunches and moved to draw the bunches out via the back seat.

"Gillian."

She whipped round, heart racing. Only because she was startled, not because Vic's voice made her heart race. His laugh didn't hide the noise of the shutter clicking as he took pics of her, half-crouched and wrestling with a multihued bunch of curling ribbon and a balloon they'd missed about to escape into the sky.

"Oh. I forgot you'd be here." Lies. Obfuscation. Nonchalant pretense.

He shrugged like he believed her. "All part of the service."

Natalie slammed her car door and joined them. Her bundle of balloons somehow looked as tidy as she always did. "Hi, Victor. Things good?"

"Sure are. Forecast for next week is great, by the way. I've got a few ideas I'll email you about for the photo shoot."

She gave Nat a look. Didn't even pretend she wasn't, because no matter how nonchalant, Vic was gonna see through her.

"I didn't tell you Victor's doing our engagement photos?"

Gillian's need to answer Natalie hovered in the negative range. All three of her best friends getting married in a six month period? Fine. Busy, but fine. She was happy for them. And okay, it made sense they'd look into the same vendors, despite how different those weddings would be. Rachel and Nat were using the same florist, and Nat had booked Serena's caterer the day after Serena's wedding. It seemed a bit much, though, for each and every one of them to have Victor Anthony taking their wedding pics.

He stepped to her and snagged the flyaway balloon. Tied it to her wrist like they were kids at a carnival. Reached behind her to shut the car door. Smelled like lemon with an inky, metallic undertone.

"Okay, gotta get this lot inside," Nat said, chirpy as fuck. Gill wasn't letting her get away with that. She spun away from Vic and marched behind her scheming friend, all too aware of the balloons bobbing in her wake like a pastel manifestation of every one of her turbulent emotions.

ANTON WOULDA TOLD her to lighten up.

Or made some bad science-adjacent joke, more like. Told her to inhale some of the helium from the balloons so she could float up away from her bad mood.

Once, he'd have been just as likely to tease her as her little brother. Back when it seemed wisest to pretend she was like a sister to him, too. All part of the pretense of belonging to the Bellamy family unit. The lighter-than-helium dream of fitting in with Anton's over-invested, high-expectations, rules-and-chores-and-order household.

Not that his folks neglected him, exactly. Not that he wanted for food, clothing, shelter, or benign good wishes. Even now, they texted like ... well, not like clockwork. Like a little wind-up toy with a mostly-reliable spring mechanism. All part of the free range parenting that might have suited someone like Anton just fine. If Ton had been left to pursue his own interests, he'd still have topped the charts in his favorite classes, and earned competitive scholarships, and never feared the consequences of coming out, to boot.

Vic, though, got through school because Mr. Bellamy kind of scared him, and life would have been miserable without Anton to ground him in the reality of their daily lives. So he tried to not disappoint the man, for fear he'd no longer be welcome at the dinner table. Be told to get his toothbrush out of the striped cup by the sink. Be labeled a Bad Influence.

Looking back, neither his folks nor the Bellamys were so very extreme. And he and Anton had planted roots deep into each other's corner since the day they'd sat at the same second grade table and the boy at the next table called them the Tony Twins. His kid perspective, though, was a confusion of being always adrift and worried and determined to cling to the rock of Anton's family.

So even once he was old enough to notice and name his crush on Gillian, he didn't deviate from the role of extra little brother. Weekly sleepovers with Anton were more important than youthful fantasies about girls too old for him anyway.

Now, though? Now he weighed the bedrock of his friendship against the possible soaring heights of a relationship with Gillian, and wasn't ready to resign himself to the idea that he couldn't have both.

"Let me get the door."

It wasn't a little-brother joking, but it did stop her in her tracks. Irritated as much at his words as at her friend for going inside without her, would be his guess. She gave him such a sarcastic smile, almost enough to catapult him fully back into their later teen years. Back when any kind of offhand notice from her would fuck him right up for the hours more he'd be spending surrounded by her family. Too bad for her he wasn't that always-horny kid anymore. Now he was all about nuance.

"You look great, by the way. Don't want you to think I'm so distracted by your balloon halo I don't notice that dress and that lipstick."

Pursing her raspberry-dark lips at him, she turned fully to face him. "Not buying this innocent act, Vic."

"Whose innocent act you mean? Natalie's? Yeah, me neither."

"Oh, don't worry, I have words for her, too, later."

"You got words for me, Gillian? I'll take 'em. Lay it on me."

She just looked at him. Narrowed eyes, shifting jaw.

"Or actions, if your words got lost somewhere in your big brain. I'm told they speak louder than words, even ones as adept and erudite as yours."

"You should consider shutting up, Victor Anthony. I'm not fooled by this whole 'who me' pretense you're shoveling out." She accompanied her statement with a flourish of her hand at him, likely not considering the way it made the balloon he'd tied to her wrist bob against the rest of the bunch.

He smirked as at least five bright orbs bounced into the back of her head. And took a picture, cause that was worth at least nine thousand of her super smart words.

CHAPTER SEVEN

RACHEL: Up for doing us a favor today?

She texted Rachel back. Because she was, for once in her life, a few essays ahead of the grading game.

GILLIAN: What do you need?

RACHEL: Since it's such a pretty day and we've got the kids, Nat thought we'd like to horn in on their picture time at Bayou Bend

GILLIAN: Okay...

RACHEL: But they'll be dressed up so I don't want them to have to wrangle the kids

GILLIAN: You're making up an excuse for me to be around Victor

RACHEL: No! We really need help w the kids! If you're free

Gill could call her on the transparent setup, if she was into pointless wastes of time. Or she could flat-out refuse to join them at the stately historic home and gardens where her best friends congregated.

The sky stretched cloudless and azure out her window. And the redbuds lining her neighbor's sidewalk pulsed purple with spring blooms. And it would be fun to chase the kids up the low grass steps between the classical Diana fountain and Bayou Bend's back veranda.

Never mind her friend's obvious schemes. Getting the most out of the prettiest time of Houston's year was worth it. Her decision had nothing to do with the way Vic's eyes—and lens— had taunted her from across every space during the party at Elixir the week before. Or with his actual taunts, daring her to consider him in his own right. Not as the kid he'd been, not as her brother's friend. Not even as the man who'd been notably attuned to her pleasure, that one time back in college.

Long ago now, she'd decided those memories weren't to do with Vic being such a great lover. Just that most of the guys— and some of the gals—she slept with in her college days weren't all that good yet. She'd been with plenty of mind-blowing partners in the decade since Vic, so there was no reason to put his potential naked time skills into any kind of internal debate about what to do about him.

GILLIAN: Fine, tell me when

RACHEL: :)

Natalie and Evan would be all gussied up for their engagement photos. Rachel and Theo would coordinate Andres and Hannah for their family portrait. But she wasn't going to be on film, and she wasn't showing up to signal any kind of interest in Vic. So her yoga pants and university tee were plenty acceptable attire.

And everyone knew about her lipstick collection. Picking a shade that matched the deepest fuchsia of the azaleas that would be in vibrant bloom fed her own joy. Because her own joy was her priority. That, and being present for her beloved friends on an uplifting, warm and vivid February day. She threw a water bottle and the bubble wands she'd picked up for the kids in her bag and set out to prove her indifference.

"EYES HERE, MAN."

Vic turned back to Evan, who was openly laughing at him. So was his fiancée. Couldn't blame them, since they were supposed to be his focus, as they stood together at the top of the brick path in the butterfly garden. Problem was, he'd heard a kid calling out, "Gillian, this way!" Which had to mean any second now, his second clients of the day would arrive, with Gill in tow.

"Sorry." He waited for Evan's smirk to transform into a smile just for Natalie, who leaned into him and made some kind of noise Vic couldn't quite hear from his end of the pathway. Whatever it was, it put a knowing and loving glint in Evan's eyes, and Vic proved to himself that he could be plenty professional even when he was distracted by the way his body was thrumming in anticipation.

As bad as being seventeen and knowing he'd find Gillian back from college for a visit when he went to Anton's. He crouched, intent on forcing his body to work with the well-known demands of photography rather than the fizzing awareness of Gillian's proximity.

Everything came to a halt when Rachel's crew arrived. Lots of hugs and mutual admiration and general acting like they hadn't been at a party together just five days earlier. The kids did the expected and took off along the whorls and dips of the rough brick path delineating the butterfly. The adults clustered together watching them and admiring the neat boxwoods and profuse azaleas making up the butterfly's wings.

He stood behind his lens, observing. As always.

Theo waved him over. "We're going on a bit of an exploration to let these two bounce a bit of energy out. Meet you by the fountain in a bit?"

He nodded. "Maybe fifteen minutes? I want to get Evan and Natalie in the white garden while the sun's like this."

Maybe the guy understood what he meant about the dappling through bright green branches overhead. Maybe not. Either way, he nodded and took the kids in hand. Gillian was sitting on a wrought-iron bench with Rachel, who waved off her fiancé and their kids. Vic allowed himself a few moments of taking her in while he packed away a couple of lenses and shouldered his reflector.

"Ready?"

Caught again. He looked at Evan, aiming for a face that wouldn't give himself away. The man's crow's feet didn't persuade Vic he'd been successful.

"Yeah. There's a wood bridge over this way, let's see if it's busy."

Evan nodded, but didn't make a move. He scrunched his face and glanced at the women on the bench, making room for Natalie to squeeze in with them. Then back at Vic. "So. Are you into botany?"

Vic raised his brows. "I mean. I like plants. The colors, the overlapping textures of a formal garden like this. The way trees gather themselves into layers to reach they light they need when they grow close like that." He gestured at the tangle of trunks sloping down towards the bayou beyond.

Evan nodded. "Sure."

Vic nodded back.

"What about coffee?"

"Am I into coffee?"

Another nod.

"It's fine. I'm more of a soda person for caffeine, I admit." He followed the man's gaze and clocked the way Gill slapped her hands over her face. "Do you like coffee?"

"Nat and I, we met at a coffee shop. Not by coincidence. Our parents set us up, and that's where we picked to get the meeting over with."

Vic grinned. "Bet they're pretty smug about that."

Evan shook his head. "You have no idea."

He hitched the camera bag again. "So. Ready to move on?"

"Sure. Of course." Another glance at his betrothed. "What about sports?"

"Evan. Have you been sent to interrogate me?"

The guy blushed. Vic tried to hide his amusement, putting on a patient expression as he waited for an answer. One last look at the three women, all now with heads cocked in their direction, and Evan broke. "Okay, it wasn't exactly my idea."

"But you were so subtle and smooth."

"Argh. Shut it. You're the one who's obvious about being into Gillian, so don't cast subtle aspersions my way. We just figured we should get to know you a bit, if you're going to get all caught up in her."

"And knowing I prefer live oaks to pin oaks helps with that." He nodded. "I see."

"Deflect away. It doesn't change the fact you've been staring after her every time we see you."

"If you don't think I'm doing the job—"

"Nah, come on, it's not that. Dillon keeps texting pics of him and Serena posing in front of the framed pics they've got up from their big day. No one questions your skills. Just your intentions towards our friend."

He deflated. Both cause Evan punctured his near-blow up of professional pride, and cause: Gillian. As if his intentions ever mattered to her. "You don't need to worry. She's not the one who's going to end up hurt in this scenario."

Before he could turn fully away, Evan clapped a hand to his shoulder and squeezed. "Oh. Sorry, man. I get you now. And for the record, you ever want to talk about it? Or just meet up for a drink? Text me, okay?"

He didn't look back to see what kind of non-verbal nonsense happened behind him. Just nodded and led the way deeper into the gardens, because whatever came next in his intentions towards Gillian, he had jobs to do and no intention of fucking up the one thing he knew he could control.

CHAPTER EIGHT

RACHEL: GILLIAN ITS TIME

Gill didn't even pretend to her class that she wasn't checking her phone. Volume on, special tone for Rachel's texts, and screen turned face-up on the lectern so she could see the flash of the incoming notification.

She texted back immediately.

GILLIAN: You gorgeous brilliant woman, I'm calling you in five minutes. No, Theo. I'm calling Theo in five

RACHEL: Chill. Finish your class. These things are only 8 minutes apart

GILLIAN: You all-caps texted, I'm not finishing class

RACHEL: Knew that would get your attention

GILLIAN: Have you told the others

RACHEL: Just about to. Wanted to let you know first so you don't run screaming from all your confused students

Gillian: They're perfectly capable adults. I'm sure they'd survive.

Still, she took a moment to look at the thirty-three people scattered among the seats in Lecture Hall 47B. "Y'all have any questions about the assignment?"

A couple of them did. And she deserved each and every one

of her teaching awards, so she answered thoughtfully and completely and threw in a bit of research advice, to boot.

"Anything else, email me. I'm going to go hover at the hospital while my godchild's being born."

She left them to their packing up and headed straight to the parking garage. This time, she was ready. She hadn't been prepared the last time, when Rachel had Hannah. Even after the birthing classes, and reading online advice, and helping pack the hospital bag, she hadn't thought through her own hours on the maternity wing. Dead phone, uncomfortable shoes, bland cafeteria food: not again. And, sure, this time the baby's father would be the main support, but that didn't mean Gillian was taking it easy. She'd stashed a backpack of essentials into her trunk a month before Rachel's due date.

Once at the maternity ward, she hugged Theo tight and handed him a bottle of water. "Let me know when you want me to tag in."

He blinked rapidly. Licked his dry lips.

"Come on, don't get all dazed on me. Sit down for five minutes. Text an update to your folks." She shuttled him to the chair beside Rachel and handed him a protein bar.

"Thanks. No, I ate earlier."

"How long ago earlier?"

He glanced around, then at his phone. "Breakfast?"

"You didn't eat breakfast," Rachel said. "Did I tell you about the dad at daycare who had a seizure while holding his newborn, since he hadn't slept or eaten since the night before?"

Theo groaned, but tore open the wrapper.

"You play mean," Gillian told her.

"You taught me well."

"Damn straight I did. Where's Hannah?"

"Preschool," Theo said. "Depy's picking her up."

"You want me to instead?"

Rachel squeezed her hand, but not in a 'oh hell this contraction is ripping me up' way. "Stay here. You can pick her up in the morning and bring her over, assuming I'm through all this by then."

Gillian watched her best friend's abdomen ripple and heave. Rachel barely flinched. "Are you on the good meds already?"

She nodded. "Got the epidural twenty minutes ago. Seven centimeters, baby!"

They grinned like fools at each other. It was notably more relaxed, and even fun, than when she'd been the birth coach for Hannah and neither of them had had a true clue what to expect.

Her phone bleeped. "Serena and Nat are here. Want to say hi, or leave them outside?"

The nurse shot her a look, but this was Rachel's show. If she wanted to fill all available floor space with a three-piece orchestra and a dozen jugglers, it was her choice. "Sure, give them the room number. I won't kick them out unless they're toting barbecue and reminding me I can't eat anything."

"One brisket sandwich. Three years ago." She looked at Theo. "This woman can hold a serious grudge."

"You don't have to tell me." He moved back to Rachel's side. "She remembers everything. It's amazing how brilliant she is."

"Flatterer."

Gillian turned away. Mainly to give them this intimate moment before they welcomed the child who would create the physical link between their other two children, making them all a family of the blood as well as of the heart.

Partly to look out the window for their friends.

And just a minuscule percentage of the emotion gnawing at her heart had to do with the way Theo knew Rachel as throughly, after not even ten months, as she did after ten years. Knew the things that made her feel vulnerable, and shored up her insecurities before she could even have them. Knew the times she needed a hand, and the times she had to move on her own. Knew not to bring high-aroma food into the damn delivery room, but to expect a long grudge about it if he did. His thorough love for her seemed amplified with every scrap of knowledge of her he gained, and Gillian didn't want to think about how that kind of love was something she didn't have.

———

ONCE IT WAS GO TIME, the friends retreated, to the labor nurse's obvious relief, leaving Rachel and Theo on their own.

"I heard about your romping through the daisies with Vic the other day," Serena said.

"Beg pardon?"

Natalie pointed at her. "Stop trying to play innocent. The guys have their own group text, you know."

She blinked dry eyes. Damn hospital air. "You mean with Victor?"

Nat snorted. "Not just yet, no. Evan and Theo and Dillon."

"Yep, and Dillon spilled each and every bean about your couples' day at the gardens."

"It was not couples' day. Not even close. I was helping with Hannah and Andres, is all." Never mind how she'd ended up staying at Bayou Bend after everyone else left.

Everyone but Victor Anthony.

"Uh-huh. And that's how come he kept staring at you every second he wasn't taking our pic." Natalie pulled the smuggest, most told-you-so face in her vast repertoire.

"Just like he did at our wedding!"

"You should have been too caught up in your special day to notice any such thing," she grumbled at Serena.

"You think I can't bask in bridal bliss while also paying attention to one of my BFFs and the guy who held her in some kind of movie-star clench to kiss in the New Year?"

Nat fanned herself like the waiting room wasn't sixteen kinds of over-air conditioned. "That was one hot kiss."

Gill checked her phone. Just in case Theo needed her to go back to the delivery room for some reason. No messages from anyone but her dean about spring break. "First off, that was three months—and two days—ago."

"But who's counting?" Serena asked, like she didn't know exactly how many days she'd been married.

"And on top that, it was New Year's Eve. Kissing at midnight is just tradition."

"So is copping a feel, and burying your nose in your partner's neck, and spending the next three months hyper-aware of every move she makes, I guess," said Natalie.

"And circling the man all the next day like he and you had magnets attached to your naughty bits," said Serena.

"And taking more photos of you than of us at our engagement shoot."

"He did not." Gill studied Natalie. "How would you even know that, anyway? You left before he was taking my pic."

"And Evan and I met him two days ago to choose our save the date image. But good job admitting to being his favorite model, very honest of you."

She tried to derail the conversation with talk of their save the date e-card and the problem with the printer for the actual invitations, but to no avail. Serena and Natalie both kept coming back to asking her about Vic. Serena even pulled up the screen shots Dillon had texted her of the chat between the men.

"Do they know he does that?"

Serena shrugged. "Why would they mind? They aren't saying anything scandalous. And they know we share everything anyway."

"Know you and Dillon share everything, or know the four of us share everything?" And did they see the import, to her, of the difference?

Nothing at all coy about Serena's grin. "Both."

"Wait." Natalie raised her eyebrows. "I thought I was the only one reading the guys' text thread."

"Do they read our texts?" Gill wasn't nearly as sanguine about all this sharing as her friends seemed to be. Even less so when both women nodded in unison.

"Not always. But sometimes it's just more convenient," Nat explained. Like that was eminently sensible, all this convo between partners when she thought it was just between friends.

Gillian pinched her brow and closed her eyes and did not think about how each one of her best friends now had entire dimensions of their lives that she was lacking.

Or, not 'lacking.' That implied she wanted what they had. Absent. Absent wasn't as dire as 'lacking.'

Well, fine. They could all—husbands and fiancés included—gossip about her and Victor and anything else they wanted to keep their conversational balls juggling. Her life was more than full. Friends. Students. The personnel committee. And, any minute now, a new godchild to treasure. At no point in her thirty-plus years had she chosen to define herself as lacking, and she wasn't about to start now.

CHAPTER NINE

WITH GROANING RELIEF, Gillian shut down her computer and packed up all her empty food containers and the draft chapters of the book she was crafting out of her Ph.D. thesis.

"Doing anything exciting over the break?" asked Fred, looking up from his desk in the office across from hers.

"Exciting for me. I'm taking my goddaughter to the rodeo. And the zoo. And we're making ice cream." And putting her to bed and building towers and any other activities she and Hannah would dream up during their week-long staycation.

"Sounds ... domestic."

Fred seemed a little more startled than was flattering. But it was true that she'd never really talked about how much time she spent with Hannah. She dug out her phone to show off pics of Hannah and baby Cassandra, and explained her offer to keep Hannah during her spring break while the new parents worked on getting the occasional bit of sleep.

"Cool. That's sweet. Listen, though. This is too awkward, but I promised I'd ask. And if I do it now when we're about to not see each other for ten days. I can pretend it never happened."

A soupçon of wariness crawled up her spine. "Ask me what?"

She'd never seen Fred blush so hard that his skin glowed.

"You remember meeting my cousin at that film screening at the museum?"

She cocked her head. "The documentary about the cave paintings?"

"No, I wasn't at that one. The French Comedy Festival."

"Oh, right, yeah. Ronnie, was it?"

"Roger."

"Roger. Yeah, sorry."

Fred snorted. "I'm the one who sorry. Thing is, Roger's been pestering me about you. Asking if you're single."

"Well. I'm ...." She stopped. His question drew her up short not because she minded Fred trying to set her up, but because as soon as he asked, she had an immediate thought: that one kiss over three months earlier. The mere idea of her relationship status flooded her mind with images of a certain bald photographer. She hoped her knee-weakening mental leap towards Victor Anthony didn't register on her face. Fred was an expert on nonverbal communication systems. Last thing she needed was to visibly flounder in front of him.

"The entirely correct answer is that I'm single right now."

"So, there is someone." He nodded like she'd spilled every leaf in an entire tea store's bulk bin aisle.

Damn her expressions and his ability to read them. She temporized. "Roger seemed like a nice guy."

Fred's nose wrinkled in a message she was able to interpret perfectly well.

"Or not?"

"Nah, he's nice or I wouldn't have asked. Just maybe still more of prankster than I expect at his age."

She shrugged. "Nothing wrong with a good prank."

"Depends who's doing the pranking. But you're right, he can be fun, and I do think you'd get along." Fred knew perfectly well the types of people she dated, even if they'd never talked specifics. He'd been at enough of the same events with her and her rotating collection of men and women. Not that she always brought dates to work functions, but when work overlapped with her and her date's interests, like the film series at the museum, she didn't see any reason to avoid bringing them along.

"I respect that. Tell him—well, I don't know. Tell him not now, anyway." A part of her wanted to disavow the words as soon as they were out. And not because she wanted to create a wider opening for Roger; it was the thought of putting a deadline on her vibe with Vic that threw her.

"So the upshot is you're taken, but if that changes, you'll let me know. Sounds fair. Meanwhile, I can put this entire conversation out of my head and pretend I'm not going around pestering my colleagues to date my relatives like some sort of babushka."

Gill raised her brows at him. "Babushka?"

"Babushka, Auntie, someone like that."

She hitched her bag over her shoulder. "It's no crime to be immersing yourself in traditionally-female emotional discourse, Fred."

"Don't lecture me about outdated gender roles, Dr. Bellamy. Remember—you told me all about your parents."

She threatened again to ask about switching offices next term. He raised a perfectly skeptical eyebrow her way. Smiling, she tapped his doorframe. "Have a good break, Fred."

"Hey, you, too, Gillian. Enjoy the zoo."

"I'M NOT EVEN sure why I'm invited to this thing," Vic told Anton.

"Because you make friends as often as you breathe?"

He tossed a ball of socks at Ton's chest. Somehow, even though Vic had lived in the same house for twenty-eight years, while Anton was hardly ever in his half of the duplex he co-owned with Gillian, a good chunk of Vic's nicer clothes were stashed at his friend's place.

And most of them needed washing. Anton tossed the socks

into the hamper he'd carried into the spare room with a sarcastic amount of ceremony.

Vic kept digging through the pile on the bed. "They're not supposed to be my friends. They're clients."

"Tonight, they're friends. You're off duty."

"Am I supposed to be making friends with my clients? Is there any ethical problem? Or is it expected? Should I have been making friends from all the people who hired me for the past two years?"

"Don't spiral. Wear the green shirt."

"Which green shirt?"

"The one in the closet. How is anything on your bed actually clean?"

Vic nudged the clothes to a neat mound against the foot-board and sank to the mattress. "I don't get why you gave me a room here when I have my own place."

Anton glanced past his shoulder and didn't answer.

Shit.

"I don't mean I'm not glad. You know I'd sleep here whenever you're in town anyway, if you didn't get sick of me or I wasn't interrupting your love life."

Anton's lips pursed. Signs that things with Cisco—he presumed it was still Cisco—were taking an interesting turn. Vic would dig into that if he had time before he was due to leave for Evan and Natalie's joint bachelor-bachelorette party.

"Fine, never mind me. I'm taking my uncertainty about tonight down a road I know will lead to you telling me I'm the best friend you've ever had and ever could have and I can just ask you to say that instead of picking a fight about it first."

Ton cut his eyes at Vic, but didn't answer.

"Right. And you're my anchor in the world and I could never find a more dependable or steadfast friend and the day you sat next to me in Mrs. Crawford's class was the most important day in my life."

That earned him a grunt. Damn but he loved Anton beyond words.

He threw himself at the closet and flipped the hangers until he unearthed the green shirt. Anything to cover the flush of nerves invading his chest. *Fuck*. Gillian had hinted at the agony that would result if anything shook the Tony Twins apart, but it wasn't like he'd ever considered it possible. No way, no how would Anton dump him. Not even if he and Gillian got together and it didn't work out.

Like it wouldn't work out.

He knew what he wanted. He knew it was the best idea for all three of them—him, and both the Bellamy siblings. Anton would be all in for the relationship. Vic would get to be with Gillian. She would be happy being with him. He could make her happy.

"Tony?" He tucked his shirt in and turned to face the guy he knew better than anyone. Including, on far too many levels, himself.

"Tony." Anton leaned against the dresser.

"Best friend no matter what, right?"

Anton nodded, holding his gaze.

Vic was the one to look past him, at the wall that divided the Bellamy homes. He caught himself gnawing on his lip, which was a habit he thought he'd killed back when they were in middle school. "What if ... you remember that time in college?"

Anton looked over his shoulder, as if he could sense his sister getting ready for the same party, just a dozen or two feet away. He turned back and nodded. "Course."

"What if I need to try again?" He spat it out and dared to shut up and wait for an answer.

"You sure it's a good idea?"

The spot on his sternum where his camera often rested suddenly felt bruised. "You don't think it's a good idea?"

Anton moved to the bed and started shoveling the clothes pile into the hamper. Not answering.

"It's not just a crush anymore, you know? Not like when I was a kid. And I've thought about it, okay? Made sure who I am now and who she is now, that there's the connection there. A vibe that's as real as anything, more than I've had in years. Like Della, or Holdyn. Okay, not Holdyn, but with Charlotte, you know? But it's more intense than that for me, this time. *She's* more. I don't—"

Shutting up wasn't ever something he'd been good at. All their lives, he'd been talking and Anton'd been listening. Or lost in his own thoughts, content knowing if it was super-important or hilarious, Vic would get his attention.

So it wasn't at all common for Anton to be the one to interrupt. "You were never into Della. You just thought you should be because your parents introduced you."

Damn his shaved head and the absence of any hair to pull in frustration. "I'm not talking about Della anymore."

"You thought it would make them pay more attention to you if you were with someone they liked so much."

"Anton. I don't give a shit about Della. Or my parents' opinions about who I'm with."

"Not anymore. But you did. You thought whoever you dated would get them to love you better."

He was seconds away from literally banging his head against the wall. "For a hot second when I was twenty-one, maybe. But that's a million days ago."

"Not even three thousand days."

Great. He tripped the man into math mode. "Fine. Three thousand. Whatever."

"Victor. Shut up. I'm making a point."

When Anton used his full name, Vic shut up.

"Your parents were never going to love you more for dating Della."

He continued shutting up, because what the actual fuck?

Maybe noticing that Vic wasn't the epitome of a thousand watt bulb switching on, Anton made the connection for him.

"Vic, they weren't going to love you more cause they already love you as much as they possibly can. Who you date doesn't make them love you any more, and who you don't date doesn't make them love you any less."

His sternum still ached, but he—maybe—got it. So long as he wasn't projecting his own wishes over reality. He cleared his throat, trying and failing to create a path to let his fear-tinged words emerge.

Anton pushed into his space, narrowed his focus just on Vic. "Victor. I am never going to love you less. It doesn't matter if you date Gill or stay away from her or if you break each other into three thousand pieces down the line. I'm never going to love her less, and I'm never going to love you less."

He cleared his throat again, enough to croak, "Thanks, Ton. Same, you know?"

"Of course."

He nodded and rubbed his hand over his scalp.

"Now stop spiraling. And also, this is your room forever, but maybe take ten minutes to straighten it up before you go declare your even-more-than-Charlotte feelings for my sister?"

He thwapped Vic in the forehead and sauntered out, whistling an old cowboy song they'd made up rude lyrics to when they were ten, leaving Vic to wipe his eyes and smooth his shirt and start a load of laundry.

CHAPTER TEN

MOST TIMES, she didn't hear much from Anton's side of the building. Not even when he had guests. Their master bedrooms were separated by their closets and bathrooms; their living rooms by closets and stairwells. But if she was on the stairs or in the entry way at the same time as someone in her brother's duplex, voices carried. Not just the fact of them, but the individual tones.

So she knew if she opened her door just then, she'd find Victor Anthony talking to Anton in his entryway. And it would be ferocious cowardice and unnecessary delay to hover in her house until Vic departed. They were both headed to Nat and Evan's party. Seeing him right there in her doorway was no different from seeing him in twenty minutes in the wine room of the snazzy restaurant.

Not different at all.

She glanced at the hall mirror. Not that she expected to look strikingly different from fifty seconds before, in her bathroom. But damn her if her expression would give away that she'd felt her heart spike and spark once she heard Vic's voice through the wall.

Cool as the April evening breeze outside, she stepped onto the porch. "Hey, guys."

"Gillian." Anton surprised her with a hug. "Have fun tonight."

"You sure you don't want to come? Nat told me to ask you seven more times to be sure you know she means it."

He retreated to his threshold. "She knows it's not my thing."

"She does," Gill agreed. "And she apologized for Evan having a ridiculously large batch of friends and family."

"I'll forgive her, but if this marriage doesn't work out, I expect her to marry an introvert only child next time."

Vic's laugh compelled her to look at him. Whatever kind of bulb they had in their porch lights was in lust with his skin.

Or maybe that was her nonsense eyeballs. Either way, ridiculous. What difference did it make if his shirt hugged his shoulders and the bulge of his biceps? She saw his forearms plenty when he took photos. The way they stretched all lean and strong out of his rolled up sleeves was nothing new.

She made her voice neutral and natural. "You want to get a lift over with me?"

No call for him to smolder and glint when he nodded. "Sure, sounds great." He turned to Anton, who surprised her again by wrapping Vic into his arms.

She wasn't eavesdropping. But this was her baby brother's voice, the one she'd spent more of her life attending to than any other. The one she'd been parsing for decades, learning each nuance, careful to know all she could in her determination to never make life an iota harder for him than it already was.

So she picked up the fierce truth of it when he pressed his head to his friend's and said, low and intent, "Never going to love you less, Victor."

It was all she needed to forget every nuance of Vic's musculature and his intent eyes and whatever ridiculousness her heart suggested when she thought about an extra twenty minutes in his company. Because never mind Cisco, never mind how Anton's feelings for Vic fluctuated from brotherhood to beloved over the years; the bare fact was that the Tony Twins needed each other. And she couldn't bear to disrupt the balance between them with her random, unnecessary ideas about getting Vic into her bed again.

HE HELD HER DOOR. Before they set off, once they arrived, going into the bar.

She ignored him, much as she had during the drive—banal chitchat and some history of her friends' various romances. Not a hint of that bright intent he'd sworn had met him at Anton's before they set off.

So. What changed? Nothing with him, for damn sure. Not with Anton's understanding and encouragement shoring him up. Making him fly faster towards the light that was Gillian. Hopefully not like a damn moth, about to be crisped beyond recognition, but willing to risk it if so.

He put a hand on her back as he ushered them inside, and she stepped away. Fast. Maybe to grab Natalie in a hug. Maybe.

Okay, he would regroup. And never mind Gillian being his favorite person in the room. In almost any room. He would get to know Evan and Theo and all them. See how that furthered his cause.

Or the cause of friendship and so on. Anton assured him it was fine, so he wasn't going to move past the superficial bonhomie that marked his friendships with everyone but the Bellamy siblings.

Lots of mingling, lots of drinks, lots of appetizers and laughter and more mingling. And then Evan gave a loud whistle and everyone gathered round where he and Natalie had positioned themselves in front of a table holding a pile of bright postcards and little mesh bags.

He ended up across from Gillian, who took one look at the

table and tilted her eyes at a grinning Natalie. If he'd had his camera ... the Nikon D850 would do such sharp and luminescent work of the light and lines before him.

She narrowed her eyes even more his way, as if she could tell how he was committing her to an indelible image in his mind's eye.

Evan said something quiet to one of his coworkers, then turned to the crowd. "So, first off, thanks everyone for coming out to party with us tonight. We are pretty excited about next weekend, but experience—also known as too many married siblings—taught me that Nat and I won't have much of a chance to just hang out with people during all the pomp and circumstance."

"That's for graduations. You're thinking of the Mendelssohn. *A Midsummer Night's Dream*," Natalie interrupted.

He kissed her cheek. "So right, as always. And even though it won't be midsummer, marrying Natalie is definitely a dream come true."

Everyone went *aww* and cooed and made other such expected approving noises.

"You're such a sap. Is it too late to call this whole thing off?"

Evan's emphatic reply was echoed by Natalie's friends—Serena, Rachel, and Gillian the loudest of all.

She shrugged. "Fine, then. We'll get married. Finish your speech." Her pretended nonchalance was adorable, and Vic couldn't stop imaging having such easy banter between him and Gill. Or noting the way Natalie and Evan touched all the time. Not lewdly, just constant connection, communicating with each other above and beyond the way they did with their crowd of guests. He'd like that, too.

Evan's whole face was playful and smug. "So, way back in the murky mists of time—a dark and depressing time, from all I'm told—some foolhardy person ghosted on Natalie."

Serena tossed an ice cube towards Evan. "She was with him for years!"

"And I forgive her that terrible lapse in judgement," he said. Then jumped a little, squinting over at his betrothed, who raised eyebrows at him. "Ouch. Okay, okay, point is, all these extraordinary and brilliant and mindful and beautiful and talented and—ouch! Woman, I'm complimenting your best friends, you are supposed to be putty in my noble hands!"

Natalie snorted. Vic envied the way she expressed every emotion she felt around Evan, like there was nothing she could think or feel that would impede their connection.

"So the four of them got together, and came up with the most prescient and foolproof plan to predict their future loves. They made a game board—Serena's masterful artwork at its best, as y'all can see." He held up one of the postcards, which Vic could now make out as a grid with pictures in each cell.

"When did you start saying 'y'all,' bro?"

"Best gender-neutral pronoun in existence," Nat told one of her soon-to-be in-laws.

"And lots of time talking to a lot of Texans," Evan added. "Point is, they made this game board and everyone took turns rolling dice to find out about their perfect match."

Evan's smug look echoed across to Dillon and Theo and their partners. All those happy couples, and Gillian the only one not in a relationship. Vic glanced at her, but she showed no evidence of minding how goo-eyed all the couples were.

"One of the many ways I swept Natalie off her feet—shut it, Brad—was with my prodigious poetical talent. Not to make any of you singletons here swoon, but I've written one to share with you all tonight."

Nat leaned in to whisper to him. His cheeks tinged red. All the smug was on her face, now.

He cleared his throat. "Anyhow. Raise your glasses to toast to the end of our single days." His voice took on even more of a bounce as he recited.

"Since no other guy was quite nice,
Nat took a big chance on the dice.

Each roll did reveal
A man so ideal—
When she met me, she didn't think twice."

Vic joined in the laughter and cheers, suddenly glad that despite his awkwardness and hesitation about crossing the work-friend divide, he was spending time with all these people. He joined in the effort to pass the cards and bags out to everyone in the room. People gathered in clusters, occasionally hooting about some of the options on the fortune telling grid. At least, most of the guests were—leaving just Gillian, Natalie, Serena, and Rachel, together with their partners, standing around the table.

And him.

Before he could think of retreat, Dillon handed him a card and bag. "Don't want you to miss out on your ideal."

"Ah, the ever-generous Rocket Man," Gill said.

Dillon was the blushing one while his wife said, "You can say that again."

"Okay, y'all might need to explain a bit more to me." Vic studied the card, first clocking the picture of the rocket ship, and then reading its column heading: *SEXYTIMES*. Oh. Maybe he didn't need an explanation after all. He opened the mesh bag and found a six-sided die, a condom, and confetti shaped like shamrocks and horseshoes.

Lifting his chin, he caught Gillian's eye. And bit his cheek at the uneasy look on her face.

"So, I gather Dillon was the rocket. Also, what, blue eyes, and ... the computer for the job?"

"Pencil," Dillon corrected. "And one sibling, but I don't have a dog or a motorcycle so the thing's not perfect."

Serena nudged him.

"Not perfect at predicting me, I mean. But it's right that we're perfect for each other."

"Damn straight," Serena said.

"What are you?" Vic asked Evan.

"Dollar sign, of course, since I'm a banker. Black hair. Five siblings."

"And a tiger, for sure," added Natalie.

He growled. Then they kissed. And they kept kissing.

Rachel poked Nat's shoulder. "Did you put condoms in these to make fun of us?"

Theo grinned. "A good precaution for all the other lightning bolts like me out there." Vic must have looked confused, because he added, "Much as we love Cassandra, she wasn't really part of the plan."

"Nothing about you was part of the plan," Rachel grumbled, but Vic photographed couples for a living; he knew a tight connection when he saw it.

And that left him blinking at Gillian again. Wondering if she could see his wishes in his expression. Wondering what she'd rolled in their game. Wondering if there was any chance he fit the bill.

CHAPTER ELEVEN

Somewhat or another the man always managed to be looking at her when she wasn't trying to look at him. Also, he was closer. Serena and Dillon had retreated into an intimate huddle, and Vic flowed into the space they left.

"What about you?"

It would be childish to ignore him. "What about me, what?"

"Yeah, what was it you rolled again, Gill? I can only remember the hamster."

She crossed her eyes at Rachel, who wasn't even trying to act like she wasn't taunting her. "I don't know why we even put a hamster on there. Far too ridiculous."

"You don't happen to have a hamster, do you, Victor?"

Her look told Evan he'd be lucky to make it to his wedding, but he just crinkled his nose at her.

"Nope. But back when we were kids, I wasn't allowed to have any pets, so Anton pestered his folks until they got him one, and told me we could share."

Wait, *what*? "Samster was your idea?"

Everyone else laughed at the name Samster the Hamster, but she was waiting for Vic to confirm. "I mean, I wanted us to get a llama, but your parents wouldn't go for that."

She tried to imagine her parents fielding a request for a llama. Couldn't even get past the picture of her nine-year-old, quieter-than-Samster-ever-had-been brother broaching the topic. She shook her head. "Anton always would do anything in the world for you."

The sour kick from Evan's custom cocktail was wreaking havoc with her heart rate. She excused herself and retreated to the restrooms. Ran cold water over her wrists, did some box breathing. Checked the stalls were empty before jumping in place a couple of times. Ran more water over her wrists and patted the back of her neck with a damp paper towel. Glared at her too-wan expression as she reapplied her plum-hued lipstick.

The thing was: sure. She was attracted to Vic.

He was attracted to her.

They both knew that. But she also knew better than to risk of shattering the bond between Anton and Vic—or between Anton and herself—by acting on that attraction.

Buoyed, she stashed her lippy in her bag and headed back to the gang.

Or tried to.

Vic leaned against the doorway leading to the private party room, arms crossed like she needed to remember what his flexed arms looked like. He wasn't going anywhere, wasn't talking to anyone. Was just watching her approach.

Well, she was the one with the doctorate asserting she understood communication. So, fine. "Hi."

His gaze traversed her body, her face. Her freshly plum-glossed lips. "You rolled a five."

"I—what?"

He opened his palm to reveal the die, plucked the game board out of his shirt pocket. "On this."

She shook her head. "Most of the rolls were twos. That's pretty much all I remember. Hamster and all."

Consulting the final, sexytimes column, Vic's lips curved into a soft grin. "Angel, huh?"

"Can you image anything more tedious and holy? No wonder I don't give that thing any credence."

"Tedious? Gilly-Bean, if that's what you resign yourself to, you are so missing out."

Damn his ability to lay in that touch of sweetness that banished the lingering acid in her heart. She made a point of looking past him to the crowd still having fun just past where they stood, apart, in some kind of battle she was not best placed to win. "Not that it's your business, but I'm not missing out. So, if that's all?"

"Nope."

Why she let his single syllable root her in place, she didn't know. "Nope, what?"

"The five." He lifted the game card again. Like the original wasn't hanging in the dining room of Serena's house for her to see any time she wanted.

"Remember thirty seconds ago when I didn't give that any credence? Same thing was true back when we made it, and every day since. Stop acting like that five means anything."

"Can't help but notice I'm the only bald man in that crowd."

"Seriously, Vic? You are aware I date people who aren't in that room, right? Sometimes they're even bald. Or redheads, or have green hair."

"You've dated someone with green hair?"

She shrugged. "Okay, 'dated' is a strong term for it, but there was a coffee meet-up once."

"Never made it to cocktails, huh?"

"She was the big sister of one of my students. Nice, though. And bisexual like me. I can set y'all up if you want."

"You may not be as hilarious as you think, you know."

"Yeah, well, you may not be as charming as you think."

He shook his head, which did nothing to lower the intensity of how he watched her. "I don't claim to be charming. I get along with people, they find me easy to hang with, but it's not charm.

Just part of that chameleon thing where I had to learn to fit in anywhere."

He didn't add anything about how his folks never gave him much of a space to fit in with them. How he was the good son archetype when under the Bellamy's roof, the actor with bonhomie in the theatre department, the on-time employee at the campus bookstore, the steadfast goalie of the intramural team.

How she had to know it wasn't easy for him to risk disrupting his one point of personal security with all this intent, seductive teasing.

But she did know. She knew all of it, because she knew Vic. Even without all the stories from her brother over the years, she knew what mattered to him.

She swayed forward enough to take the game board from him. There, in the first column, that bald head. It had been her first roll. She never mentioned it, but the moment that die turned up a five, she'd flashed into an image of Victor Anthony. She hadn't needed to check that five was for baldness; that's how fast she'd associated that space with him. With her.

With them.

Looking back at Vic, she stroked her fingers up the inside of his wrist until they tickled across his palm, caught on the edge of the die. As she pinched it up, he wrapped his hand around hers.

"I never admitted it, but." She licked her lips. Caught him watching the move. "I might have wanted to roll the five."

His fingers flexed. They'd slid right up against each other. "If I'd been there, I'd have run off to get you a weighted dice just to be sure of it."

That damn green shirt of his. He should use fabric softener to stop it reaching out of its own accord to grab ahold of her bodice. Forcing their bodies to touch with only the barrier of some clingy fabric between them. Bringing her heart perilously close to his.

"I rolled for a ball, too. Thought I'd conjured up a football player. Maybe the coach on campus, he always seemed like a nice guy."

Something flaring and daring flashed in his eyes. Maybe it was a trick of the venue's ultra-modern lighting.

Maybe it was a reflection of her own thoughts.

"I don't think that was it," he said. "I think it was fate reinforcing how much you wanted it to be me. Ball, bald. Just one letter apart."

She swallowed, which was a ridiculous tic that had no place in this intense stand-off of theirs. "That's far-fetched."

"As far-fetched as the lengths you're going to deny there's something between us?"

"I'm not—" Her instant protest died as he curled a strong arm around her back, lifted her hand to the back of his neck.

Kissed her.

Not just kissed her. Kissed the hell out of her.

CHAPTER TWELVE

ENOUGH OF HER TEMPORIZING. He needed to touch her. Taste her. Teach her how serious he was.

It had been over four months since that New Year's Eve kiss, and every day since he'd wondered how to make it happen again. And again. And more agains until they both lost count, until no kiss was such a stand-out that he could recall its particular circumstances.

But this one, he would always remember. This one, with her plum-ripe lips and her floating curls and her flowing curves, all brushing and baiting and beguiling him. Her taste. Her spark and spirit crashing into him as they touched.

Because Gillian Bellamy was touching him. Not in a 'fine, it's tradition, let's just do this' way, but with intent. Finger spreading up his scalp, legs crowding him back against the wall, mouth as sure on his as his was on her. And her teeth, nipping at his jaw and his earlobe. Her hums of pleasure reverberating in his torso, spreading a shiver-thrill through his limbs that felt like he was breaking out in goosebumps all over. Even his dick quivered, pulsing fast as he hardened against her.

He didn't notice the noise of the party behind them, or the clink of normal business around them. But he wasn't so caught up in himself and the moment that he minded when Gill broke their embrace to glance around and adjust them into a less private clinch.

"Hi."

His heart thudded at her simple, clear, unwavering word. Not running. Not downplaying. Looking at him like she meant every nuance of that syllable. "Hi, yourself."

"Want to get out of here?"

Best six words he'd ever heard. "Hell yes."

They went to say goodbye, and didn't answer any of the teasing questions, didn't touch each other until they were back in her car.

Before she turned on the engine, he took hold of her hand. "I want to sleep with you, Gill." Not that he thought she needed the clarification. He was beyond obvious, but there was no need for pretense between them. They weren't going to get anywhere unless they communicated, and his plans involved them getting lots of places. Getting everywhere, if possible.

"Ditto."

God, if she only was answering his thoughts and not his words. But he would take what he got. For now. "Your place okay?"

She finally looked at him. The streetlights burnished her with amber and made reading into her expression a hell of a task. But he'd known her for two-thirds of his life, and just the way she tilted her head while leaning easily against the seat back was a clear sign to him. "My place is fine. And don't think I missed how you grabbed extra of those party favor condoms on our way out."

"Didn't mean for you to miss it."

"Or anyone else in the room, either," she grumbled.

His grin contradicted his shrug, but he didn't care. "I can't help it if they draw their own conclusions."

"Brat." But there was no heat in her tone, just a fond caress he felt to the soles of his feet. She started the car and didn't stop him from lacing together their fingers once they were in the flow of traffic heading home.

By the time they were on her porch, they'd both let their hands explore everything in reach of the other. Or, almost everything. They kept it just shy of PG-rated. He traced up her arm and over her shoulder, then down the sweet soft sweep of her side. She circled his knee and ran arabesques up the length of his thigh bone, ending with a squeeze that taunted but never touched his aching cock.

He wasn't paying the slightest bit of attention to the door abutting hers, but wasn't quite lust-fogged enough to miss the way she pinched her lips together as she noted Anton's glowing front windows.

"Hey." He gently turned her head his way. Kissed her, because kissing her filled him with the kind of golden-hour light people put up with gnats and humidity and exhaust fumes to capture on film.

She relaxed into him, which was all he'd hoped for. And more. All kinds of places it hadn't been wise to touch her while she drove, he could touch now. All kinds of undistracted sounds and scents and sweetness, with her tight close to him.

He pulled back enough to whisper. "Inside?"

She nodded and lifted her keys towards her lock. He'd never been more pleased to see an unsteady hand, but it wasn't like he was rock-solid enough to help her. In maybe nine seconds, he'd gone from someone with super-trained solidity to someone who needed at least a third of his body in contact with hers for him to stay upright.

But then again. She swung the door open and he saw the stairway and all his strength rushed back with one intent: get the woman up to her bed. They rushed in, kicking off their shoes, throwing the deadbolt behind them, unbuttoning his shirt.

Everything in him boiled up the stairs, rushing and pounding. Took him a sec—okay, a few seconds—to notice that some of the pounding wasn't theirs. Boot heels storming down the stairs through the dividing wall. A slamming door. A shout of frustration that would be an ironic echo of his internal state, if it hadn't triggered an automatic turn towards worry about Anton. He was back on the ground floor, re-buttoning his shirt, before he blinked to the realization he should be focused on Gillian, not her brother.

WELL, that chilled her fervor. One moment she was all in, shelving her concerns. The next she was pushing Vic down the stairs ahead of her. At least he didn't impede her. He covered up those strong pecs and tucked his shirttail in like he was on board with her need to restore the two of them to the point where she could find out what made Anton holler like a run-over coyote.

As if the scrunch of Cisco's truck tires backing out wasn't clue enough.

"Shit. Sorry, Gill."

She quirked her head. Did he plan to stop her checking on her brother? Was that why his hand was on the doorknob?

"I didn't mean to rush away. It's not that I don't still want you. This was kind of knee-jerk for me, you know? We can ... just head back up to your room." He dropped his hand, turned to face her. Offered a half-serious eyebrow wiggle. "I am more than ready to do anything you demand to get back in the mood."

Wow. Okay. So instead of him feeling abandoned, he was abandoning her first. Good info to mull over. Later. "No. Let's head over there."

Before she could slide past all the warmth of his body and open the door to clear her house of the smell of his dark flower cologne, he traced a finger across her brow and cupped her cheek.

Kissed her.

It wasn't enough to make her forget about Anton. But it also wasn't enough to make her forget her reckless intent to get this virile man into her bed. Into her body.

"You good?" His damn sincere gaze studied her.

"Never better." To prove it, she reached down to squeeze his butt, then hip-checked him out of her way. "Let's go."

The six steps between her front door and Anton's was plenty of space to regain control. Good thing, too, since Anton yanked his open as soon as Vic's shoes sounded on the porch.

"It's just us," she said, and watched her brother's shoulders slump. He didn't say anything, but didn't shut them out as he retreated to his sofa.

She and Vic took their customary places on either side of him. Shoulder to shoulder to shoulder. She felt Vic's prompting nudge as it waved through Anton's body to hers.

Not that her brother responded.

"So, the party was good. We're just back from it."

He ignored her.

Vic tried. "And I found out Gillian is superstitious."

She snorted. "Am not."

"Are too. You're convinced your fortune teller thing is fate."

"Don't be full of shit."

"Telling it like it is."

"Telling yourself what's convenient to you."

"You know I'm right, Gilly-Bean."

Anton ignored them both, and she flushed hot at how much they weren't helping her already-hurting brother. He didn't need their flirty crossfire on top of whatever had happened with Cisco.

She took his hand. "You want to tell us what's up?"

Vic wrapped his arm around Anton's back, and she shut down the shiver that hit her when his fingers tickled at her. Last thing she needed was to transmit her unresolved sensations to Vic via her brother.

"That was Cisco leaving in a huff, right?"

Anton snorted at the obvious answer to Vic's question.

"You know we're here for you," she said, giving his lax hand a squeeze. Like she could press words up his arm, past his throat, and out into the living room. She needed to get on with fixing whatever happened. It wouldn't be the first time, and it wouldn't be the last. It was her job as big sister to the best guy in the world. He couldn't communicate well; she had a Ph.D. in Linguistics. They complemented each other.

But first she needed to understand the problem.

"Did he hurt you? Cheat? Say something cruel? Make fun of you? Steal? Sabotage your job? Post private pics? Give you an STD?"

She barely clocked the withdrawal of Vic's arm until the sofa jostled. He pivoted to sit on the coffee table and put his hand over where she held on to Anton. "Gill, that's a pretty extensive list to just rattle off the top of your head."

He watched her all wary, like she was a skunk meandering past his campsite.

She shrugged.

He looked at Anton. "Has all that stuff happened to you or something?"

Her traitor brother shook his head and discovered how to talk all the sudden. "Not to me, no. But I never knew about someone giving you an STD."

She wanted to yank her hand out from between the two of them. "He didn't. No one did. All my screening tests have turned up negative, thanks for asking."

"Who tried to change that for you?" Vic's voice held a growling menace she wasn't used to.

"No one, relax. And my dating life isn't the point. We're here for Anton."

Now it was her brother trying to pull away, but Vic tightened his hold on them both. "Tony."

That was all he had to say, and all the tension slumped out of her brother. "It wasn't any of that stuff. Y'all don't need to worry. I'll be fine."

Vic cut off her next barrage of questions. "Ton. Hey. Tell me something."

He sighed the same sigh he'd given in childhood, when their parents quizzed them on verses Anton's quick mind knew cold after one reading. "Tell you what?"

"Tell me how many times now we've talked about some problem of mine, and you minded me needing your help?"

Anton shook his head. "Zero."

"Right. And now tell me how many times in the past twenty years I've minded you needing me."

"Not the same."

"Bullshit it's not the same. Was I or was I not spiraling in your spare room—"

"Your room."

"Fine, was I spiraling in my room up there not three hours ago?"

He was? Obviously he was, or he wouldn't have used it as proof against Anton's reticence. Not that her brother conceded with more than a shrug. Singularly unhelpful to her need to know why Vic was a mess before the party.

"Right. So. What happened with Cisco and do I need to kick his ass or what?"

Anton managed to extract himself from their hovering and moved to the door. "No, you don't. And I'll tell you about it. Later. I'm going after him now."

"Let me drive you," she said, reaching for his keys.

Vic got there first. "You have work to do in the morning. I'll drive him."

"Don't need either of you to drive me."

"And we don't need to be up for hours worrying about you traveling up and down the freeways all upset. Come on." Vic threw a glance at her before steering Anton out the door. She was left on the wrong side of the duplex, at a loss for how to interpret about five dozen of the night's moments. And even more of a loss trying to grasp what she wanted the answers to be.

CHAPTER THIRTEEN

GODDAMN COWARDICE and problematic muddled feelings. She actually peered out the window of her study to check if Vic's SUV was outside before making her way to her brother's.

"So, what all happened with Cisco?"

"You're not going to lead up to it any? Just ask?"

"I'm the one who taught you how to ease into a topic. You're the one who finds it a tedious convention."

Anton side-eyed her. She'd taught him that, too. She was a truly excellent sister.

"Okay, fine. Did y'all find him last night, at least?"

He nodded.

She waited.

He picked up his book.

"Anton. You were so upset last night." Her chest went tight again, remembering. Decades, now, of wanting to soothe his upset. Of being the best at it, so her parents and everyone turned to her first when he needed it. Of helping him figure out the best ways for him to navigate his emotions. Never mind that he was grown now; the urge to jump in and fix things for him never went away.

But to fix things, she'd need details. And for details, she needed Anton to speak up.

Or she could ask Vic, but that ... that felt unsavory. She wasn't about to start some sort of Anton Support Club with him, not any more than they already had just by being his two main people. In all their decades of supporting Anton, they'd never gone around problem-solving behind his back.

She wasn't sure how things might change because she and Vic got steamy with each other, but one thing they all agreed on: neither of them would change their independent relationships with Anton. So prying at Vic for what he'd learned about this Cisco situation was a no-go.

According to some rule-bending part of her brain, none of that stopped her from talking to Anton about his best friend, though. "Why was Vic spiraling here before the party?"

Her brother marked his page and paid her some attention. "I thought he would tell you."

"Well, I haven't talked to him."

"Why not?"

She didn't want to answer that. Mainly because she wasn't entirely sure. Unless she was afraid she would accidentally pump him for info about the search for Cisco.

Or because she'd gleaned that Vic's tizzy had to do with her, and she wasn't quite comfortable with the idea of him being invested enough in their ... relationship ... to get into a spiral about it. Which would mean there was such a thing as a relationship happening in his hearts-and-roses-filled mind.

Not hooking up, not a fling. A relationship. Coupledom. Commitment. To the wedding photographer who exuded his love of happy-ever-afters all over every one of his clients. To the man who'd spent years ensnaring himself into the bosom of her family, and would, she suspected, covet the opportunity to make those ties more solid and legal.

"Have you talked to Cisco today?"

"Am I supposed to be distracted enough by your topic change to answer without thinking?"

She snorted. 'Distractible' had never been one of Anton's attributes. Even in those toddler years, when other kids could usually be redirected, he'd stayed focused on what he wanted.

"No, I just figured you're not going to talk about Vic, so I went back to the reason I came over." And also she hoped changing the topic would quell the squirming in her gut.

Anton snapped his book down on the coffee table. "I talked to him last night, when we tracked him down."

"Where was he?"

"His sister's house. Even though her kids were all in bed."

Ah, okay. She could take what she knew of Anton and intuit the problem. "He wanted you to meet them?"

"That's what he kept saying."

She watched his beloved, mulish face a moment.

He pressed his lips together. "He introduced us to his sister and brother-in-law. And a cousin. And his uncle."

"You and Vic?"

"Yeah."

"And how was that?"

Anton eyed his book like it would be a casual kind of escape from her questions.

"I don't think Cisco would care if his sister's kids don't take to you right away." Or at least she suspected that would be the case.

"He has eighteen videos on his phone of him playing with them."

She shifted to curl up on the sofa facing him. "Did they strike you as needy, whiny, entitled brats?"

He side-eyed her again. She loved him so much.

"So logic dictates that they already have an uncle who they have fun playing with, and won't need to demand you entertain them."

"Your version of logic needs work."

"Ha. Deal with it. Because unless Cisco said he'll end things if you don't charm his sister's kids the minute you walk in her door, I think you can trust him to let you find your own way of relating to them. Even if that way is from a respectful distance."

"Kids don't like me, Gillian."

Her gut wrenched again. It was the most pervasive and least proven thing Anton believed. "First off, Hannah thinks you're hilarious."

"Hannah thinks everyone is hilarious."

"No she doesn't. Did you know every morning she was here last month she asked when we could go to your house?"

He dropped his head back and stared at the ceiling. "Well, she's known me her whole life."

"And second, how many other children have you spent time with since you were one yourself?"

He closed his eyes.

"Not to be all 'you're not so special' here, but pretty much every kid at some point has trouble with their peers, and with self-doubt, and with feeling like they don't fit in. Not for all the same reasons as you, but I don't think there's anyone who doesn't bump up against some of that. And I know lots of kids in those situations are glad to have met adults who accept them as they are."

His snort-breath told her she didn't need to say her next line, but she did, anyway.

"Like the adults you met at the rodeo."

Everything else, he could sort out for himself. He didn't need her to lead him word by word to the conclusions he'd already have drawn. And she didn't need him to acknowledge what they both already knew: that his fears of being rejected or ridiculed by Cisco's nieces or nephews were based on old wounds and not on current evidence.

"Vic said it's a good sign if he wants me to meet his family."

It was her turn to flop her head onto the sofa cushion. "Yeah?"

"Something about folding me into other corners of his life. Sharing me with them because I'm important enough that he wants his family to be able to envision me when he talks about me."

There was Vic's ultra-romantic streak again. He was always seeking ways to grow the circle of people who adored Anton. He'd vet them first. Or befriend them, she supposed. Any rate, if he trusted them, if they would be good to her brother, Victor Anthony fostered connections that brought more love and acceptance into Anton's life.

Her only problem with that particular drive of his was her worry that what Vic really wanted, when he kissed her, was a way to fold himself forever into Anton's family. And no matter how he made her tingle and spark, she'd spent enough of her life not quite measuring up to Anton to let that be the driver in her love life, too.

It wasn't that she didn't kick ass. Obviously. She was proud to claim all her external markers of success: doctorate, journal articles, tenure-track job, sparkling peer and student reviews. Each an extra bandage around her fluttery tiny heart of fear.

But she always had this ... kernel of fear. Of not being adequate. Of not mattering enough. Of comparisons. Because all of those little bandages weren't enough to stop the blood from seeping through. Would she ever rate highly in her own right? Be more than adequate?

Seemed unlikely.

Seemed even more unlikely, sometimes, that she could prove it to herself. All of those markers of success were good external validation, but no one saw how much work it all took. How much forcing herself to get up early and draft, or fall asleep planning strategies to engage a lecture hall, or hours supposedly chilling over a movie actually ignoring said movie in favor of scrolling job postings and calls for upcoming conference papers and lurking online to see what her peers were accomplishing.

It wasn't comparing herself to those peers that cut at her. She knew she couldn't see their struggles or insecurities. But she'd never managed to stop comparing herself to the idealized Bellamy in her head. The one that combined her ambitions and interests with Anton's ... everything else.

If Anton had her job, he'd have published in every journal he submitted to. If Anton had her job, he'd host a podcast and lead a progressive student group in addition to teaching. If Anton had her job, he'd have gotten into the one doctoral program that had rejected her, and been fully funded, and been offered tenure before he even had to defend his thesis.

Never mind how unrealistic any scenario was, a part of her just knew that if she was Anton, it would have happened.

And she didn't, deep down in her fluttery tiny fear-heart, treasure the things she had that Anton wanted—or might want if his brain was wired differently. Didn't care that she couldn't know a thing about how he'd have done in her position, on her path. Didn't care if she loved all the things Anton didn't have that she built easily for herself—her friendship group, her easy rapport with her colleagues, having people she could vent to without worrying she was going overboard or being hyper-focused or using up every last scrap of their patience.

So she was greedy on top of everything else. On top of inadequate, and afraid she'd taken the wrong path all her life. and petty. and jealous, and bad at prioritizing.

Inside, she was leaping around like a pathetic child needy for attention, screeching 'look at me, look at me, look at what I can do' and bursting into pity-party tears when it didn't work. When her ambitions outstripped her abilities. Because she wasn't Anton, so the world didn't approach her saying, 'I see you, I see your value and what you've been doing. I want you to submit to me, I want you to come work for me, I want you to lead up this panel, I want you to keynote this conference, I want you to bless us with your presence, your name, your brain, your company.'

And she had to live with that, just like always. But she could still draw the line at letting Anton be the main reason someone wanted to date her. Better to stay away from Vic entirely than to let his devotion to her brother—and his romantic nature— inspire him to turn their chemistry into a romance that didn't take her own fluttery, bandaged heart into account.

CHAPTER FOURTEEN

FOUR DAYS since he'd led Anton out into the night while sending a surreptitious text for her to call him, and how many words had she bestowed on him? Six. Two monosyllabic texts. And if he knew one thing about Gillian Linette Bellamy, it was her fondness for what her father referred to as her ten-dollar words.

So, yeah. He got the message. He didn't know why she'd sent it, but he got it.

He was tempted to ask Ton, but ... it felt wrong. Felt like cheating. Or tattling. Either way, like regressing. Being fourteen instead of twenty-eight.

He hired Jorge to assist with Natalie and Evan's rehearsal dinner, too, instead of just their wedding. Not that he strictly needed it, but he wanted the extra cover in case he needed to corner Gill during the party. Or to at least keep him on task if she continued to freeze him out. Cause try as she might to make him feel like an awkward teen, he was a fucking professional.

Despite the monologue rant in his head. He proved it by capturing great images of the engaged couple and their moms. Of the groom's many in-laws laughing like they'd been in on a successful conspiracy. Of Gillian, surrounded by her friends, not even pretending to be unaware of him capturing the love between them all.

Fucking invisible, that was him. Not a blip on anyone's radar, so in a week or two when Natalie and Evan would go through these shots, they'd be amazed his lens saw so much when no one saw him.

No one ever saw him. It was the job. And he didn't need Gillian to even blink his way for him to do his job. She had no problem forgetting his existence? So be it. More proof he was worth what he charged.

Jorge came up behind him and rubbed his shoulders. Cupped his scalp to swivel and waggle the tension out of his head and neck. "Go grab a break, man. Your ergonomics are for shit."

Great. Fantastic. Stupendous, to use a Gillian word.

He made his way to the little table by the kitchen door he'd claimed for his equipment and cases. Made room for a bowl of the kosher gumbo and basket of cornbread. No crayfish for him. Hard enough to avoid the shells and spices just navigating the room full of people shucking and sucking. And who'd have figured image-conscious and elegant Natalie and Evan would host a boil for their rehearsal? From what he gathered about the venue and vendors for the next day's reception, this was an uncharacteristically messy last hurrah before things got fancy and formal.

Speaking of formal, Gill approached him with the least casual air imaginable. Like they hadn't spent innumerable days slouched on the same sofa watching movies. Like they hadn't banded together dozens of times to talk Ton down after his folks made some cutting remark.

Like they hadn't been minutes from fucking within recent memory.

"Vic?"

He just looked at her. Waiting for anything beyond single syllables from her.

She helped herself to a chair and a slice of cornbread. "Hey, sorry I haven't called."

He raised his brows. "Are you?"

"I didn't mean to leave you hanging."

"Huh."

She crammed half the bread into her mouth. He spooned up some gumbo.

By the time she swallowed, she'd gone full glower. "You don't think it's a tad insipid, to go all pouty child on me like this? You can't deign to make an effort at mature conversation?"

Damn her for making him laugh. "It's lovely to see you again, Gillian. Are you enjoying the party? Have you been well? Have you been thinking about how many orgasms you missed out on since last we met?"

She crumbled the last of her bread into his bowl and took his spoon. "Hilarious. You're so full of nuanced wit. It's a shame you stick with a non-verbal art form."

He found himself reaching for his camera before he'd thought about it. A protective instinct born of years of amateur and professional photography.

And he wasn't going to define whether he was protecting his equipment, or himself.

"What do you want, Gill?" Besides his gumbo, which she polished off. He slid his glass of iced tea her way.

"Thanks."

He grunted.

"I wanted to say hi. It felt too awkward to be in the same room for an hour and not talk."

"That wasn't my choice. And if you didn't know that, let me make it clear. I've been making moves on you all this year because I want you. A relationship with you. Dating, being a couple, sleeping together. Acknowledging each other's existence when we're in the same room. All of that."

She returned to glowering. "Well, forgive me for not allowing you to make unilateral decisions about my life."

"Did I say it was a done deal? Did I walk in here wearing my 'Vic and Gill 4Ever' sequined t-shirt? I'm not making decisions for you, Gill. I'm telling you plain and clear what I want, and—like always, like forever—putting the ball in your court."

HERE SHE GOES and makes an effort. Makes a point of reaching out. Extends a bushel full of olive branches. And he snides about her court? Nope. No. She wasn't the one who drove off with Anton and never came knocking again.

"How am I calling shots when you're the one running out the door the second my brother calls?"

He took back his drink. "We both ran out that door. Don't lay things at my feet when you trod the same path."

"You drove off into the night."

"Which you were about to do instead before I stopped you." He looked past her. Stood. "I'm on the clock, Gillian. If you want to talk this out—and to be clear, that's what I want, so don't play like you don't know that—catch me when the party's over."

And then she was just sitting in a corner, alone, with a bunch of crumbs.

Ridiculous. Asinine. What about the fact she was a brides-maid? She had to go over details with Natalie. They all had to meet early the next day for the whole beauty routine thing. She hadn't even had time to break in the heels dyed the same lilac or lavender or whatever shade it was that Nat was calling their dresses.

Or the inclination, anyway. She'd had plenty of time. But she wasn't going to wear the heels on campus, and she didn't like wearing shoes in her house, and they didn't go with the jeans and leggings she opted to wear when out running errands.

So screw Vic Anthony and his 'catch me later' attitude. His

'we should be in a relationship' dictates. His 'the mature thing to do is have a conversation' subtext.

She had shoes to break in.

CHAPTER FIFTEEN

"So THAT'S why you left so early? Just like that?"

Gill cut her eyes at Serena, but she knew her friend had the right of it. "I needed my beauty sleep."

"First off, when have you ever cared about how beautiful you are? And second, Nat's the bride here and she was partying until two in the morning."

"She's also the hungover one right next to you. Can you lower your damn voice?"

Serena gave Nat a firm pat on the shoulder. "Sorry, sunshine. Happy birthday! Happy wedding day!"

"Go away."

"Oh, look, your mom's here," Rachel said, loudly enough to startle the infant in her arms.

"Crap." Natalie sat up and groped for her cup of coffee. "Who brought the eye drops?"

The rest of them burst into laughter, and Nat turned to look at the salon's empty-of-Elaine parking lot. "You scheming, lying traitor. Give me that baby right now."

First Rachel gave Nat a kiss, then draped a burp cloth over her shoulder. "Give her back before you get sprayed with hair fixer or foundation or whatever."

Natalie shook her head. "Listen to your ridiculous mama, little Cass. Thinks I'm going to poison your sweet sweet face before you can even focus those big eyes on me."

Cassandra didn't stir. Six weeks old and already so used to staying chill no matter how many siblings or aunts or friends tried to hog time with her. Gillian sidled up to be available for her turn. Unfortunately that gave Natalie a chance to study her for whatever truth she might be hiding when she asked, "How much are you stuck in your feelings for Vic, anyway?"

"Ditto," said Serena and Rachel together.

She fixed her glare on the bride. "I never said I was stuck in my feelings for him."

"You also never said you were a smart-ass brunette, but some things are obvious."

"Hey. Not in front of my godbaby."

"Sorry, little Cass. Aunt Gillian's right that no one should be labeled based on their appearance. Though she missed the nuance that I didn't put a judgment value on her dark hair, just noted she has it."

"Don't try to deconstruct your verbal nuances at me, even if it is your wedding day. You know I'll take you down."

"And you know I'll get right back up and ask you about Vic again."

Neither of their other friends was poised to intervene. Serena was tapping at her phone, and Rachel was taking photos of Nat holding the baby. It was the pitfall of paired-off besties: she was the only one left with a love life they could gossip over.

Not that she had a love life, per se.

"Shouldn't we be talking about you instead? On Serena's wedding day we talked about her for something like seven straight hours."

"Hey."

"Deny it all you want."

"I didn't deny it," Serena said, scooping up Cassandra even though it was obvious it was Gillian's turn. "I rejected the notion you should use it to deflect from telling us about Vic. Dillon and Jorge and he were talking while they packed up last night, and he says Vic was morose."

Gill waited for more details. None emerged.

Nat made a pouting face that was anything but bridal. "Aw, poor guy. And he's usually so cheerful all the time. So good at putting people at ease and getting them to give him their real emotions and listening to what they need."

"I know, right? Dillon and Jorge were texting about it this morning. Jorge says it isn't like him at all to be so withdrawn on the job."

One more pointed comment and Gillian would take the baby from Serena, no matter if her time was up or not.

"Anyway, in case that wasn't mentioned, this is my wedding day." Natalie stroked her newly-straightened hair and turned to stare her down. "And any minute now, my mom and Theo's mom are going to show up here and stress me out trying to outdo each other fussing over me. So it's your job to distract me from pre-stressing about being stressed."

Serena stood swaying with the baby. "Rach and Cass and me are going for our pedicures now. Get with the being a good friend and confessing to how you've been thinking about Victor ever since you first rolled that five for a bald man when we made our fortune teller."

Rachel stirred from the half-doze she'd fallen into while waiting for her turn in the mani-pedi massage chair. "Remind me to drink an iced coffee the minute she finishes her next feed."

"I will," they all three said.

"Also, remind me who it was that suggested we add 'bald' to the list of hair options."

"No one remembers that," Gillian protested. And it was true that she didn't know who had offered bald up as an option for the prediction game. Even if it was also true that her first thought, once the dice claimed her destined guy was bald, was of Victor Anthony.

PROFESSIONAL, that was him. Sending Jorge to do the bridal suite photos just to avoid one of the bridesmaids. Fussing over the light meter instead of meeting anyone's direct gaze. Having the wedding coordinator shuffle in and out the various groups alone when his normal routine was to be involved with the task.

He slid into the niche behind the DJ where they'd stashed his stuff. A quick scroll through the latest pics reassured him he wasn't cheating Evan or Natalie out of any key memories. He tagged a few shots to send the couple as a teaser at the end of the night. Grabbed a fresh battery pack. Reminded himself that Gillian knew the score now so his sidling up to her to tell her she filled his mind and he wanted her and he admired and respected and was awed by her—all that was unnecessary. Overkill.

So. He was professional. Did his damn job.

She gossiped with her friends. She snuck tiny bubble-wand bottles into the hands of all the kids. She conspired with the rest of the wedding party to surprise the bride and groom with a completely over the top birthday cake covered in confetti sprinkles and fluffy frosting balloons and firecracker-looking candles that kept relighting. It was their joint birthday, so it was a truly threatening number of flames. Gillian was ready, though, holding back Natalie's hair and clearing the fancy napkins and so forth out of the way. In the end, the various nieces and nephews came forward to help with the candles and were sent off to share the cake once Natalie and Evan shared a token amount.

It was goofy and loving and just the right touch of levity to balance out the otherwise all-elegant reception. It highlighted why the bride and groom chose their joint birthday to also be their wedding day—their connection was deeper than the beautiful facade of their lives. They trusted so much in their love that not only were they getting married, they were doing so on the day that would now forever be about the two of them, instead of either of them as individuals.

It was everything he wanted with Gillian.

And she had yet to look his way.

He knew, because professional or not, he'd spent much of the wedding with her in his lens. He had shots of her smiling, of her crying, of her looking tenderly at her friends. But nothing of her looking at him. At his camera, sure, for all the posed shots. And he knew all too well the difference. He'd been avoiding people's eyes via the viewfinder for well over a decade. So he was on to Gillian's tricks.

Dillon strode to him. "Come on."

"What?"

"Put the camera down, we need you."

"For what?"

Dillon smirked. He caught sight of Jorge's signal that he was on it. Whatever *it* was.

"Okay, you've conspired, and that's fine. But she doesn't want to mess with me."

"She's here without a date, and that was never her plan. Plus, Serena told me to do this. So, come on."

The DJ scrunched her nose encouragingly at him when he cased his camera and headed past her. As soon as he and Dillon were near the head table, she announced that the newly-weds' friends and family had another surprise for them. Dillon parked him in the gathering circle between Gillian and Rachel, then stood to Gill's other side like he was preventing an escape.

"What are you doing?"

He looked at her. "I have no idea. I wasn't in on this plan."

"Relax. It's the Hora. You'll catch on fast," Dillon told him.

"I know the Hora. And how is it a surprise? It's on my shot list."

One of Evan's brothers grinned from where he was waiting to hoist a leg of the groom's chair. "Just you wait. You'll see."

The DJ turned the mic over to Natalie's mom's boyfriend, who was a cantor at her synagogue. He invited everyone to join the outer circle, the one behind where Vic stood with all the wedding party and immediate family.

Through it all, he was beyond aware of Gillian right next to him. Acting like she wasn't searing his side. Like the hem of her purple dress wasn't flirting with his trousers. Like his hand wasn't itching to take hers, to experience the way their fingers and wrists flexed to lead each other through the circle dance.

And then they were underway, and, even better, everyone in the inner circle around bride and groom held onto each other's shoulders. He was that much closer to Gillian. Their hips twisted in unison, brushing with the beat as they moved. Dillon and Theo and a few other guys moved in to take over chair duty, but they had enough volunteers without him. He pulled Gill closer.

She tried glaring up at him, but everyone in the room was singing "Hava Nagila" or humming or laughing and she couldn't hold on to her irked expression.

Evan's dad took the mic as the music shifted. "Stay where you are, everyone. Not you, Oğlum. You and your bride need feet on the ground. We're going from the Hora to Halay, which is a Turkish folk dance, also for weddings. Keep your circles, and watch my children and their spouses to lead you."

Natalie looked all kinds of confused, but Evan whispered to her. They positioned themselves at the end of the line of his siblings, and he whipped out his silk handkerchief to wave in his far hand.

Vic glanced at Jorge, who gave him a reassuring nod. He stuck next to Gill. Finally held her hand, since the dance demanded it. Well, demanded they link pinkies, but he needed her touch, so he interlaced their fingers while they watched the demonstration. "Did you learn this already?"

She creased her brow for a sec. "I don't know that 'learn' is the right word. But we did what we could with YouTube and FaceTime."

Bless each frenetic step of the Hora for pounding out his

nervous energy and, maybe, a touch of her hesitation about him. He settled in to tease. "Can't wait to see what you've got."

She flicked their joined hands enough to bap against his thigh. "Pay attention or you'll make me look bad."

"You couldn't ever look bad to me."

Shit. Too far. Her sudden stillness, the tension in her fingers. He pried his dry tongue from the roof of his mouth, searching for a path back to ease between them. But the music was rolling, and the Lee family was in motion, showing off their footwork. It wasn't fancy. It wasn't beyond him. Didn't stop him focusing in like this wedding's invoice would go unpaid if he didn't pull it off.

Gillian's purple-toed foot tapped his. "Don't forget the extra kick."

"Right. Got it."

"No. Left." The joke in her voice washed triumph through him like he'd finally bested Anton at Mario Kart.

He got into the rhythm, echoing the bounce of the others as they sped up. Before long, the Lees began a few slick moves that his part of the circle had no hope of emulating, so they backed up to join the group clapping from the outskirts. Jorge worked toward him, handing over his Cannon EOS then gesturing he would get up the stairs for more overhead shots.

He leaned to Gillian. Kissed her cheek. "They're going to get all fancy here, I can tell, so I'm going to do my thing."

She nodded. Didn't reply, but did leave her hand on his chest a moment longer than necessary.

He took a risk. "Save me a dance later?"

That got her facing him. She bit her peach-rose lip, which kicked him in the gut, but her face smoothed into a smile. "I will."

It was as good an exit line as he'd get. He ducked under a cluster of aunts and found a place to crouch and capture the all fast-kicking, toe-tapping, heart-filling motion.

CHAPTER SIXTEEN

THEY'D DANCED. He'd joked. She'd fielded smug and nosy looks from her friends.

And then they'd gone home separately.

Not to say she hadn't been tempted to set up an assignation right then. But her conference proposal wasn't going to type itself. And if she was going to change her mind—damn, but her body voted for her to change her mind—she was going to do it because she was sure in her decision, not because his body moved around hers like a caressing wind.

What had she told Rachel, back when her friend was newly smitten with Theo? To stop making lists of everything he wasn't, and start making lists of what she desired in a partner. It hadn't been enough that Theo wasn't like her snivel-snouted ex. The essential thing was to identify her own wants and needs.

Same thing applied now.

Stumbling towards bed with Vic the previous week had come down to heat and lack of inhibition and a cinderblock-dense wall between thinking about the one night and thinking about the long term. And none of that was ... reasoned. Careful. Nuanced. Wise.

Vic could do his bouncing into her world claiming he was set on them having a relationship, but that didn't mean she had to agree. Even if the tingly parts of her wanted to bounce right back and get naked with him. Above all else, Gill worked to put her head in control of the desires of her heart. She hadn't ended up with a Ph.D. and a tenure-track position and panel discussion invites because she threw darts in the general direction of her milestones. She assessed the things she wanted and researched ways to achieve them and brainstormed the best paths for her to get there.

When Sonja from grad school got that book contract and when Emil's university tapped him to help develop a new minor program, she didn't bemoan their luck or wallow in envy. She analyzed what parts of their success were important to her, and listed ways she could adapt her trajectory to incorporate those elements.

So after Nat's wedding, she went home. Alone. Texted Vic that she would set something up with him in a few days.

And after giving her head a few days to wrest control of things, her headstrong heart up and invited him to come by so they could talk. His return text showed up before she had second-guessing time. He was bringing tacos. Her headstrong heart noted that on the 'pro' side in the list her hardhearted mind wasn't done filling out.

Every bit of her was forced to concede that take-out from Torchy's Tacos was a pro move.

But it wasn't enough to tip the scales. Lucky for her heart, the scales were already in favor of exploring a relationship with Vic.

Well, 'relationship.' Fling. A bit of dating. She mostly bought his theory about Anton's blessing. Bought that they were all three adults—inasmuch as a couple of men in their late twenties qualified as adult. And never mind how unfair that sentiment was. She'd known too many men in their late twenties over the years. Sure, they were better than men in their early twenties. By a vast degree. Less of a monolith of self-focus and short-sightedness. Far less apt to remind her of her students. Or of the afternoon she kept the gals in stitches composing the excuses several of her past dates would have come up with for needing extensions on their research papers.

She'd seen up close how Anton had grown and settled over the past couple of years. Become someone who looked past his own needs to the wider world. Whatever was happening with Cisco, she expected he would emerge whole on the other side. She didn't think he'd break if she and Vic were a thing. Or not a thing. Or a giant tangled mess, making navigating relationships for everyone fraught until they'd all gotten some distance.

So probably Vic was more adult in his approach to life now, too. And since she'd determined to have a relationship with her brother based on them both being grown-ass people, she could extend the same grace to her little brother's best friend.

Which, as her headstrong heart pointed out, meant she needed to trust Vic knew what he was about when he said things like, "Let's be a couple, let's be in a relationship. Let's have sex."

Leaving her hardhearted mind to just wrestle into submission the question of if she wanted any—or all—of the things he was offering.

———————

HE'D NEVER BEEN MORE TEMPTED to knock on Anton's door instead of Gillian's. Ton would welcome him in, pass over a beer and some napkins, and tuck into the tacos without asking anything of him. Or expecting him to voice his deepest desires. Or rejecting him.

But no.

He was here for Gillian, and Ton couldn't save him from whatever she'd decided. So he marshaled his arguments, and his courage, and knocked on her door.

She was wearing her standard not-work outfit of yoga pants

and a tee, and her lipstick color of the day gleamed like sweet honey, and he *wanted*.

Must have been standing frozen like a popsicle, cause she reached over to poke his shoulder. "You coming in?"

If the stars shaped themselves in his favor, he sure as hell was. What a sugar-stream of lust and innuendo and longing he was. He peeled all his melting emotions up off the porch and crossed her threshold.

Tacos. First thing was tacos. "Got carnitas, fried avocado, and a couple of those blackened salmon ones."

If he could magic the hunger in her expression to apply to him instead of dinner, he'd be able to relax. But he resolved—again—to follow her lead instead of starting the evening already arguing for why his plans for them were the best plans she could ever hear.

So he followed her past the cluttered, bookcase-lined living room to her cluttered, paper-strewn dining table. "Let me clear away this grading. Can you grab some plates and stuff from the kitchen?"

He found space to set down the take-out bag and moved to comply. The kitchen was, as always, the tidiest space in her house. Probably it was hard to break the habits instilled by the Bellamy parents—he'd found himself going about their after-meal cleaning routines often enough in his own home. He'd only eaten about a third of his dinners with them over the years, but their regulated systems and insistence on everyone pitching in stuck to him. And stuck in his craw, as he got into his teen years and noticed how differently his own folks treated household matters.

At least on their Catalina they couldn't keep near as much outdated junk, and they knew maintaining the boat was essential in a way they'd never considered with the house. He'd paid them not much for the house itself, when they up and decided to live on the water, but so much of his savings went into basic repairs he wasn't able to upgrade his darkroom equipment nearly as soon as he'd hoped.

He recycled the beer caps and tucked a roll of paper towels under his elbow. Gillian sat at the head of the table, a space to her right clear for him. He was watching, maybe too close, but he saw the lift of pleasure in her eyes when he entered. Couldn't attribute that to tacos—that was all for him.

It didn't suck, feeling her eyes on his body as he approached.

They paid maybe too much attention to doling out the tacos, testing the Scoville level of the salsas, checking each other were happy with their choices. He knew why he did it—he'd told her the decision was hers, and she'd hardly have faith in him if the first chance he got he started demanding she play things his way.

He could only hope her reasons didn't spell utter doom for his heart.

Gill made happy-eating sounds as she polished off a green chili and pulled pork taco, and sat back to sip her longneck. She was so relaxed, so whole in herself. So complete and complex and compelling.

And she traced his forearm with a finger cool from the beer bottle.

His toes curled, as did his lips. "Good food?"

"The best. Thanks."

"Anytime." He cleared his throat so it might seem like his voice had been caught up with spiciness instead of gruff with meaning. "I can even bring queso next time."

"Tempting." Now her voice was the one colored with meaningful hues.

"You mean that?"

Her fingers came to a rest on the inside of his wrist. She likely could feel the thrum of his pulse. "I do."

He swallowed. Blinked some bravery into his chest. Stated what he hoped was a fact. "This means you've made a choice."

And waited, breath shallow, for her confirmation.

CHAPTER SEVENTEEN

DAMN HIS BEAUTIFUL EARTH-DEEP EYES. His soft lips pressed tense together. The slight shadow of beard she wanted to stroke.

"You're so tempting."

"Is that bad? I can't dream I tempt you near as much as you tempt me. So don't go condemning me for something you do a thousand times worse to me."

Damn his smooth words. "I didn't damn you."

He sparkled at her. "Guess this is purgatory, then. You gonna be my salvation, Gill?"

"Hey." She squeezed his arm. Damn his strong arms. "I'm the one who does word play. Why are you stepping on my territory?"

His beautiful eyes, brightening at her. Hell and damnation. "I don't mean to presume. But I think you already know all about my presumption to your territory."

"Right." She separated her skin from his. Rolled discarded taco foils into a ball. "I do."

He drained his beer. "You can keep me in purgatory if you have to, Gill. But just know that's what you're doing, okay?"

His words tumbled like rockfall against the flimsy shelter where she'd stashed her heart. She realized in a rush that everything she'd been thinking for days—for months—took Vic for granted. Everything in her list was her pros. Her cons. Her stomach full of delicious tacos.

But he was more than an offering on her altar, up to her to accept or reject. Yes, he'd put himself there, put the power of deciding in her. And she'd needed that. Needed to think about where she was, and what she wanted. To know that her decisions weren't going to derail her plans.

None of that took him into consideration. Treated him like a whole soul that could ache for her response, be hurt by her delays. Recognized the risks he took by baring himself to her. For all she thought about her relationship with Anton, and Anton's with Vic, she didn't factor how Vic's relationship to her mattered. She'd only placed safety nets for herself and her brother.

Vic, though. He'd given her his truth. Allowed her to back-burner it while she made her damn lists. Didn't show except via one oblique statement that what happened next would change his life. Either way, his relationships shifted.

And the thing that felled her was how she stung for him. It was a hundred thorn jabs, made worse because she was the one who'd inflicted them. She hated that he hurt. That she hurt him. She wanted—needed—him to be able to be his joyous, unfettered self.

GILLIAN SCOOPED all the little containers of salsa into a bunch. "How about we leave all this fire and brimstone down here and take ourselves up to heaven, eh?"

His heart boomed. Success. He almost let himself cheer. "I know you're the pedantic one, but to be clear here: sex, yes?"

"Yes."

"... But not just sex? You're with me on this? In this?"

She wasn't as quick and quippy this time, but still she said, "Yes."

"Not to make you sign a contract or anything, but I wouldn't mind getting more clarity on that yes of yours before we head upstairs."

Gillian tossed one of her taco wrappers at him. "Thought you were raring to go."

"Obviously. But also, once we go, I'm not gonna want to stop and talk about intent and so forth."

"You have my consent, if that helps."

"So I gathered from when you said just now that we could have sex. Though of course you can change your mind. At any point. Just shove my dick out of you and I'll head off."

"Sexy."

"Yep. That's what they say: consent is sexy. Far as I can tell, this is what that means."

She sipped her beer, and took another taco. "Fine. What do you need to know?"

"Are we dating now?" He had approximately ninety-six other questions, but that seemed the most important.

"Takeout and fucking is your definition of a date?"

"You don't have to use belligerence as a shield, Gill. I know you well enough to get that I wouldn't be here if your feelings weren't somehow involved." He did his best to seem reasonable. Calm. "And I told you about my own feelings, so I know you've taken that into consideration, too."

She looked away, a sudden move that startled him. She took another sip before meeting his gaze again. Everything about her expression was a war between open and closed. If he had his camera, he wouldn't have been able to resist.

Instead, he waited.

"My feelings are involved, Vic." She was quiet as a distant chime, but it sounded like gongs in his chest.

He cleared his throat. "Thanks for the confirmation."

"Don't be a smart ass."

"Can't help it. My ass is real smart. You should check it out."

"Planning on it."

Fuck, but she made him lose track of himself. Not like he was so brilliant at locating his self to start with. He wanted to dive head-first into banter. Toy with her hair. Play footsie like a fool. And he would. He hoped. After they talked. "Okay, in your roundabout way you're telling me we are a couple now?"

"Dating. Not a couple. Or, I don't understand what you mean when you say couple. That sounds ... committed, to me."

Cannonball into a winter lake. Icy prickles casing him from his skin in to his core. "Do you want to date other people? Are you already dating other people? Cause I'm not, to be clear."

"No. No, Vic. Don't give me those eyes. I've deleted all my apps, okay? I wouldn't have invited you over otherwise, not knowing what you wanted to try."

"Okay. I mean, good. Thanks. Good. That's what I hoped. And I hope you'll tell me if that changes?" He sounded nine hundred times too young and cautious.

She nodded, and his breath got fuller.

"But, listen."

Like he wasn't memorizing each syllable and gesture. "I'm listening, Gill."

She put her hand back on his wrist. "I'm up for exploring this. All this heat between us. In bed, obviously. But out, too. You're already someone I like, that's not news, but I'm not promising we're starting any kind of long-term situation here. I can't .... We can't. We don't know enough about what we're like past the chemistry and the flirting and the basic comfort of having been in each others' lives for so long. Maybe it'll be all unicorns and dandelion fluff. But maybe we'll burn hot for a couple of nights and find that's all there is to it."

Victor kept himself steady, because: it was what he'd expected, right? Between her caution and her pragmatism and her whole thing about relationships that he wasn't sure if she'd ever considered had a bunch to do with the gender roles in her and Anton's family .... This was about as far uphill as he was ever likely to get with her, at this point.

Only at his most imprudent had he fantasized about some grander declaration from her. He smiled. Like Gillian Linette Bellamy was one to swoon.

"I like the part about burning hot."

"Vic."

"I do, though. Also the part where you noticed we have chemistry. Not sure what dandelion fluff has to do with anything, but, Gill? Joking aside? I'm grateful you're willing to give it a try. I know leaps of faith aren't your style, believe me. I get all that. So. I'm glad. It's what I hoped for. You're what I hoped for. Thank you."

And she shoved back her chair and ignored the stack of papers that fluttered to the ground and grabbed him by the hand.

They were kissing by the time they reached the landing, stripping as they sped up the stairs. Frantic heartbeats and flying garments and there—there was her bed. The one place he wanted to be. And the one person he wanted to share it with, tumbling at him. Head spinning, feet fumbling, heart thumping as they fell together into her room, onto her bed, kissing through to his every nerve ending.

No one kissed like Gillian Bellamy. Back in college, that one stunning night, they kissed and he knew it was special, never mind trying to tell himself it was his relative inexperience. Her relative experience. But it wasn't all skill—though good hellfire, was she skillful. There was a frisson with her, a snap and snarl and sweetness that went straight to his blood. Not just his heart, not just his cock, not just his heated neck or wobbly knees. Every platelet and scrap of hemoglobin glowed with joy from kissing her.

And it wasn't nostalgia for that college night. It wasn't the remnants of a childhood crush. It was her. And him. It was them, and the way she parried when he thrust, the way he nipped when she moaned.

She gleamed like precious metal as they stripped off the rest of each other's clothes. She glinted and grinned while extracting condoms from her bedside. She glowered when he stopped them. Stood, impatient, when he said, "Wait."

She couldn't doubt he meant it as a pause, not a halt. Not with his erection straining towards her while he was still wearing his damn socks, so much in a hurry were they to be together.

He bent to peel them off, which just showed her generous spirit when she didn't laugh at his awkwardness. He balled them and tossed them out towards the hall, taking a centering breath and forcing himself to not stare at—or touch—the perfect globes of her breasts. Or the curve of her belly. Or the arch of her neck.

"Needed to look at you. At your eyes."

He wasn't explaining himself so well, but maybe ... maybe how she'd also known him for two-thirds of his life made the difference. She nodded and switched on the bedside lamp. Weird how he hadn't even noticed they'd been operating in near darkness until then.

He cleared his throat and let himself step close enough to feel the sizzle coming off her skin. "I mean it, you know?"

Somehow his being inarticulate didn't stop her from agreeing. "I know. Me, too."

"Even though ...?"

"Even though." She glanced past him towards Anton's house, which was, this time, a relief.

"He knows, too."

The look she gave him.

His heart skittered but he told himself to stay centered. "How I feel. He's known, of course, but lately. We've talked. He ...." How to say the right words? Vic took in the strands of her hair he'd disrupted, the disarray of their far-flung clothes. "He picked out my shirt for Evan's bachelor party."

Gill let out a slow, sweet breath. Reached to trace along his shoulder and bicep. "I liked that shirt."

His voice was tighter than before. The syllables crunched out. "Hoped you would."

She licked her lips and he surged forward. Led by his cock, impatient to encounter any scrap of her skin. But also led by his heart, because: two-thirds of their lives. He knew her expressions. He caught the words in her eyes, telling him she wasn't twisted with worry about Anton right then. She trusted his thick-tongued attempts to explain how they had her brother's blessing, and also they didn't need any such blessing because this was just between them. And how he knew she craved it anyway, because one of the many things they'd watched each other do for two-thirds of their lives was to shield Anton from any number of the worlds' hurts.

And then.

Then they were on the bed, and his heart was racing and her breathing was fast, and she said his name. Just that. "Vic." Not even his full name, but it was the one thing he needed. The one syllable that showed she needed him in the same intense, shattering way he needed her.

He rolled under her, and he soared.

CHAPTER EIGHTEEN

FUCKING heaven and all the spirits lining the way there.

Victor Anthony first among them, because only a spirit of some sort could hypnotize her with his sunshine-bright, earth-deep eyes and lift her into some sort of transcendence just by placing his body at her disposal. And that's what he was doing, laying there like he wasn't a vibrating cock attached to a neat slab of lusting torso.

Looking at her like he wanted her. Like he trusted her.

Like he cared.

She broke into twelve thousand pieces and let each one of them pelt down like hail upon him, spread thirsting across her bed. Taking it all. Every kiss, every touch. Every scrape and slide of skin to skin. Even when he sucked at her clavicle, nuzzled his way to her nipple, used those strong sure fingers of his to part her folds and trace her every intimate contour, he was taking her lead.

And damn it all, she loved it.

She loved how he paid attention to her every hitch and sigh. How he checked in with her but also told her everything she did to him filled him with more lust. How he fucking *kissed*.

Gillian adored kissing, with the right partner. The warmth

and tension of it. The playing back and forth of pressure, breath, touch, taste. Lips soft or firm or lush or rough. Gentle tongues, teasing tongues, devouring tongues. It all sent her vibrating. Lifted her awareness of her partner to new levels. Turned her the hell on.

So she knew, racing Vic to her bedroom, she was in for hotness. Not based on those college kisses; those weren't anything she'd held to for years. But every day since New Year's Eve, she knew his kiss spun her in circles. And giving him free reign to kiss as they rolled in her bed? Dizzy. He made her dizzy. His touch, his taste, were everywhere. He nipped her neck and nuzzled her ear and navigated from brow to chin with light brushes of his sensual mouth. His moan resonated within her when their tongues tangled and his hands arced circles over her breasts. His smile burned past their interlocked lips as she spread her thighs wide to his questing fingers. His breath stole hers. Wrapped her air up to bundle it away along with her caution and her worries and her fluttering heart.

And that wasn't even taking into account his body. Shoulders and arms that begged her palms to stroke them. The birthmark just at the base of his ribcage—that, she remembered. Not just because she'd seen it at pool parties and such over the years, but because she'd traced it with her tongue that time in college. He'd laughed because he was ticklish, and he'd forgotten he even had the mark, and he'd thought she was heading lower with her tongue when she took the detour to that reddish squiggle a couple of inches above his faint appendectomy scar.

She had been heading lower, to a destination she'd never imagined at any of those pool parties when they were young. And she did it again, because this, too, she remembered. The way he grunted, then moaned when she grabbed his cock. The way he got harder just from the whisper of her breath across the head. The way he palmed her nape as she took him into her mouth.

"Gillian, you're killing me."

She cut her eyes to his, and he grinned.

"A good death. Go for it."

She pulled back and straddled him, leaning down to glare straight at him. "If you keep making me laugh, I can't give you a blow job."

He grasped her hips and flipped them over. "Guess I'll have to go down on you instead, then."

She moaned. Dying for sure. "If you must."

He stopped lavishing her nipple with his tongue. "It seems I must."

She let him splay her legs wide, lifted her ass so he could cup her closer. Laughed aloud when he nipped at the flesh of her inner thigh. Laughed more because his beard was a bit rough, but the stubble on his head was soft as velvet against her tender skin.

"Temptress. You smell like manna. Making me starve for you." But then he stopped talking and started exploring her with tongue and lips and, just a little, teeth. She bucked in his hands when he closed on her clit.

"Vic. More." And he knew what she meant. He knew to increase the pressure of his circling tongue, and reach a hand to her breast, and growl. It didn't take long under his attention before she flew free. His murmurs were delight and praise, and she was left without words.

Well, with only the one word. "Vic."

Smart guy, he read it as the order it was, and snagged a condom. Tucked a pillow under her ass. Licked his lips.

She moaned his name again, and then they were both laughing. He played his cock into her, and they grinned at each other. He drew back before thrusting home and she gasped his name and laughed again. How the hell did he make her laugh when she couldn't feel anything but the points where they were joined?

Refused to feel anything but where they were joined. And laughter. And, okay, some spiraling warm buzz of thrill arcing between her laughing throat and her clasping vulva. But that was it. That was all she needed to feel in pursuit of a damn good session of sex with Vic.

And *hell*, it was good. His hands lifting her that half-hitch higher while his pelvis tilted that few degrees deeper and—damn. "Vic! Fuck, yes."

"Got ya. I got ya, Gill."

He did. He did, and more. She shook apart into another orgasm and forcibly dragged him along with her. Like he wasn't planning to get there on his own. Like she twisted his arm tight to echo her cunt undulating around his cock.

She shoved at his bulk, and he flopped to the side, panting. It took too long to convince her heart to steady into a normal pace, for her fast-flowing blood to allow her face and her thighs and the tips of her fingers stop tingling.

Too long. It gave him time to prop himself on an elbow and nuzzle at her neck. To murmur her name in that sweet-rough voice. To blast a smile full of affection and joy and satisfaction at her.

She resisted being snared by his beautiful eyes, but Vic didn't care. He wrapped her in his happiness anyway. "You're amazing."

She grunted.

He smirked, which was nonsense. She didn't like people who smirked. She didn't even like the way the word sounded, and her whole thing was words and how they signified, so she was an authority.

Didn't stop him smirking. Or smizing. Or softening his voice as he asked, "You're good, yeah?"

"I wasn't faking, Vic."

He ignored her dry tone. "I know that. But we agreed there's more to us than hot sex, Gillian."

She ignored him.

"Gilly-Bean."

"I hate that nickname."

"Okay, Pickles."

"That's worse."

It was. It was an over-elaborate elementary school construct of her brother's. Gillian Bellamy to Dillian Bell Pepper to Dill Pickled Pepper to Pickles. Anton had charted it all out on the back of a posterboard, and debuted the name at dinner one night. He'd peeled the label off a Claussen's jar and cut pics of bell peppers and dill out of one of their mom's recipe magazines as illustrations.

Their mom stuck it to the fridge, even though it was an inch wider than the door and needed seven magnets to hold it in place. It stayed up even after Gill 'accidentally' smeared grape jelly across a corner. She'd never been more glad when report cards came home so they could displace the thing in pride of place.

"You know I helped him with that, right?"

Years too late, she shoved his shoulder. "Jerk."

"Don't get me wrong, only Ton's mind would have labored to come up with the idea. I just suggested reusing our science project to display it."

She should banter at him. Something like, "A thousand thanks for that." Or, "I always knew you were the devious one." Or, "I hope you enjoy waiting for my cold, cruel revenge."

But they were naked in her bed. She could spy the condom wrapper just past his hip. And it wasn't the sweat drying that made her skin grow cold. It was the visceral image of her brother at nine, scheming with his best friend. And the two of them at twelve, rolling around giggling at some terrible joke Vic made, because the only time her brother rolled around laughing was when Vic made a juvenile joke. And then, the two of them at fifteen, her first weekend home from college, and she saw how Anton's eyes followed Vic's every move. How it was more than the years of friendship that got them moving in sync to finish up dinner and get it on the table. More than being pals when Anton squeezed tight up against Vic so they could all fit on the sofa to watch a movie. She'd known her brother was gay; she hadn't realized her was totally gone over Vic.

When they were all off in college and Anton got into a relationship with the guy five dorm doors down, she figured that was the end of it. That it had mostly been convenience, falling in pup love for one of the few people Anton ever made time for anyway. His social circle was only ever as wide as Vic made it with his constant flitting from one interest to the next, anyway. So it made sense that her brother's nascent crush would land on the safe haven of his most constant companion.

She'd convinced herself he was over it. She hadn't even mentioned Anton, later, when she found herself responding to Vic's intent, if not adept, flirting during the spring break when they'd all been cleaning out her parents' flower beds and ended up spraying each other's muddy limbs down with the hose. Anton, as always, managed to garden without a smudge and had disappeared to his room as the dusk and mosquitoes settled around her and Vic.

So, fine. She'd been swayed by a couple of beers and the water tracing enticing trails down his chest. And maybe by feeling rebellious about her mother's domestic aspirations for her life while she was on edge waiting to hear about grad school. They'd made out behind the house. Climbed through her window and tumbled to her bed. She never did manage to re-attach the bug screen flush in its frame.

And the next morning, her brother confessed about a bad breakup and the fear he'd never find anyone who really wanted him. Gillian worked to comfort him, suggesting that college was a great time to explore different types of relationships, to figure out what he really wanted. Then Anton went bright red and choked on a sip of his always-bitter coffee.

Maybe she'd forgotten—allowed herself to forget—the intimate details of that night with Vic. But she'd never forget the way Anton stared with such apparent and painful longing at his best friend coming out of her bedroom that morning.

It wasn't the same now. She knew that. She knew Anton's heart was hitched to his cowboy, and he hadn't outlined his romantic future on Vic's pattern for years. But he still centered his social life around Vic. She'd been surprised when he met Cisco on his own, since half his previous boyfriends were people Vic brought into his orbit.

After everything Anton did to put his life on a keel he could navigate, the last thing she could handle would be to threaten one of his sturdiest supports. Or two of them, counting herself, because—lying next to Vic, reeling from the combination of their mingled scents, her pounding heart, her buzzing limbs. She was teetering. And if she fell, or if she flung herself at Vic in an attempt to not fall, that was twice the danger to Anton's stability, and an infinite whirl of problems he would be forced to navigate to resettle himself.

And that wasn't acceptable, and it wasn't fair, and it made the points where her limbs brushed and tangled with Vic's go ominously cold.

CHAPTER NINETEEN

He MADE HIMSELF SAY IT. "You're second-guessing already?"

She shook her head.

He didn't call her a bare-naked liar. Even though it was the literal truth.

A moment later, she shifted enough to brush their legs together again. "Okay. Some."

"Even though you second-guessed for like four months already?"

"Hey." She flopped a chastising hand onto his chest. He couldn't begin to mind.

"Correct me if I'm wrong, Professor. I've just got this theory that you and I just had mind-blowing sex and instead of that being a good thing, you went and worst-case scenarioed us to some vision of doom."

Her fingers twitched, which he had a feeling she'd rather he hadn't noticed. Too bad she'd left them lax on his body. "Okay, fine. The sex was mind-blowing."

"You don't have to sound so disgruntled about it."

"I'm not. I'm too blissed out and turned on to be disgruntled."

"But ...?" He shifted his head to see her better. She wrinkled her nose at him.

"Just what you'd expect, really. This was amazing. The tacos were perfect. Talking to you is easy and fun. You are a fucking brilliant kisser."

He huffed a laugh. "I see why you're upset. That all sounds dire."

"Shush." Another thwap of the back of her hand. "I have no complaints. I want you to stay in this bed for hours. Days, even. And maybe there's a tiny part of me that jumped to the last time we slept together and how Anton was crushed after even though he didn't say anything. And it's not your job to run your love life in a way that protects him."

"Not yours either," he interrupted. Emphatically. Because they'd done that before. Sure, anything could have gone wrong with them trying to fumble into a relationship back when they were college kids. But she'd cut them off at the ankles just because she'd decided Anton couldn't handle it.

"Ouch."

He flopped back and took her hand in his. "Gillian. I get it. It's a thing we both do—look how we raced to him the other day. But don't you think he's not needing us to protect him from what we're feeling anymore?"

She hummed a non-answer.

"Why can't you believe him when he says we should go for it? Why do you think he's bluffing?"

"Anton can't bluff."

"Well, he can't bluff us. I get the idea he's good at it with anyone else."

She nodded, the pillow shuffling beneath her. "Probably so. But no, he can't bluff us."

"And he told me he knows how I feel about you. He told me I should let myself feel it."

For another moment she was quiet, her hand squeezed to his.

When she spoke, her voice was thready and raw. "I know. I believe you. But. He never told me."

Oh, hell. She was not at all in the mood to face an upwelling of emotions.

There was no one—no one—she loved like she loved Anton.

Not Rachel, Serena, or Natalie, though they'd sustained each other in every travail and triumph for all their adult lives. Not her goddaughters Hannah and Cassandra, though she was prepared to cut down twelve thousand men to protect them, and also destroy the patriarchy so they'd find it easier to thrive.

Not her parents, who—even if she was around—would express their same adulation of their son. Gill couldn't remember the time before him. Her parents claimed she pitched some only-child jealous snits when Anton was an infant, but her first memories involved hovering over his bassinet stroking his soft cheek with just her pinky like her mom taught her, and somersaulting across the dining room so he would clap from his high chair, and the time she decided to take him for a walk and got him into the stroller and down the front walk before their mom came racing after them.

Maybe that last one was a false memory, after all the times their folks pulled it out as a party piece to commend how fast she went from toddler snits to sisterly devotion. Point was, he was woven tight across her living memory. A pal once snarked about Gill's whole family coddling Anton, but she hadn't been brainwashed into some kind of brother's keeper situation. She just really loved the kid. Enjoyed his solid, accepting presence. Respected how he'd worked all through school and into adulthood to find ways to fit into the world around him. Admired him for achieving so much in his career at such a young age.

When he got his signing bonus for the firm out of grad

school, and she'd just taken the university job, it was his idea for them to buy the duplex together. They hung out most weekends, if they were both in town. Raided each other's kitchens and bookshelves. Had a shed full of shared camping equipment.

She wasn't his best friend, she knew that. Anton loved her, relied on her, but she didn't compare to Vic.

Still, she thought she counted. She thought they talked. She thought if there were things to be said about her hooking up with his best friend, Anton would say them directly to her.

Vic broke into her mope. "You asked him?"

She blinked moisture into her eyes. "What?"

"Did you ask Anton what he thought about us? Did you mention to him that we'd been kissing?"

"You did?" Her mouth was a little dry, but likely that was from all the athletic sex.

"Well, obviously. How else could I get his opinion?"

Great, now she had to add chagrin on top of the jealousy and low self-worth. A real slog of positive feelings, that was her.

This was why she opted out of deep emotions, given the chance. The bad always accompanied the good. And was always more of a pain to process.

She sighed. Rolled to face him and get caught up in those pretty clay-and-clouds eyes of his. "You win. I'll put aside my grump and revel in the part where we just had mind-blowing sex."

He provoked goosebumps by smoothing back a hunk of her hair. "Gill. You're allowed to grump. I don't expect you to put up some false front of happiness just cause we're having all this stunning fun in bed."

"Don't brag."

"Ha. You want bragging, just wait another ten minutes or so."

"Promises, promises."

"This is the advantage of a younger man, you know. You'll see."

He was so cute when he smirked. It was obnoxious. She

kissed him. It was a fuck-ton more energizing than dealing with whatever melange of nonsense was swirling in her head and heart. And when he flipped himself over her and pinned her to the mattress with his body weight, she settled in to enjoy the fierce pleasure of their bodies smashing with intent.

CHAPTER TWENTY

HIS ALERTS POPPED up a slew of positive reviews from Natalie's and Serena's weddings. From the couples, from some of their families, several from the bridal parties. He rolled from his buzzing phone to look at Gillian, snugged against his back. She was feigning sleep.

Maybe she'd fool someone else, but he'd grown up sleeping over at her house, tagging along on camping trips, knowing her brother better than any other human. And Gill feigned sleep the exact same was Anton did when he hoped to get away with not being the one to fetch water to the campsite or set the breakfast table.

"Did you tell all your friends to five-star me?"

Her lips twitched like she was struggling to not laugh.

"I guess you told them about my five-star performance in bed, too? And that prompted them to rate my professional work?"

She gave in. Buried her head under his propped-up arm and guffawed.

"I mean, don't get me wrong. I appreciate the up-votes. But your friends know I'm not gonna sleep with the rest of them, right? This top rated dick is yours and yours alone."

She shoved him to his back and attacked. He didn't put up a single defense—she could do as she liked with him. Whatever her plans, he expected he was gonna like them, too.

Later, replete but hungry, he pressed for an actual answer. "I really appreciate the online kudos, you know. It just surprised me to get all of it at once."

"We should have been doing it all along. Anton told me you're trying to get to some tier or prize or something?"

So they did talk about him some. At least enough for Ton to share about his ambitions to become promoted on a popular wedding planning site. "They highlight the vendors with great and numerous ratings. I mean, there might be more to it—I advertise with them, which can't hurt, and I got some advice off a forum about ways to optimize my website and stuff. But it seems like the ratings and reviews are the most important thing."

She hummed some kind of understanding and agreement.

"You know all this already."

Her grin proved he was right. She sat up enough to bare her chest; he took his time to enjoy the morning light gleaming on her curves. "You more interested in ogling me, getting some breakfast, or interrogating me about who I talk to about you?"

"All of the above." Mainly the first, of course. But she knew that. And he was feeling secure enough in their connection to anticipate more ogling in his future.

Gill kicked back the rest of the sheets. His mouth watered. She laughed. "Come on. I picked up some plantains the other day, they're just right for boiling now. If you chop the peppers and shallots I'll scramble up the eggs."

He watched her saunter to the bathroom, then went to investigate how widely scattered his clothes were across her house.

CURSING the impulse that had led her to send a furtive, too-giddy three a.m. group text, Gillian shut down her phone so she wouldn't be tempted by all the notifications.

If only she could shut down Vic's inquiries as readily.

"So, these reviews?"

She shrugged. Dug some bread out of the freezer for toast.

"I appreciate them, don't get me wrong."

"Do you want cheese on the eggs?"

"Nope. Do you have half-and-half for the coffee?"

"Am I out?" She glanced from the stove to check him bent into her fridge. "In the door?"

He backed out and checked. "Ah. Sorry, eyes skimmed right over it."

"Cause it's not one percent?" She snickered, even knowing it barely worked as a pun.

"Hey." He wrapped himself around her. He was cold from the fridge, even through her shirt. She relaxed into him, feeling the warmth of her back equalize with the cool of his torso. Their bodies were a compatible system, working together to create comfort in the other.

She shut off the stove flames. "This is all ready." He moved to grab their plates and hold them while she filled each with their breakfast.

Probably it was all those dinners and weekend sleepovers that trained them both in how to work together at mealtime. Her parents raised them—including guests much less frequent than Vic—to be prep and cooking and clean-up helpers. No one in the Bellamy house would get called from playtime to join the family table, or excuse themselves, leaving their dirty dishes on the table, either. If Mom was in the kitchen, everyone was in the kitchen.

Maybe not Dad. But everyone else.

And ... all that self-reflection snickered at her when they moved to the dining room and viewed the detritus from the night before. The taco wrappers and container lids in a jumble at the center of their cleared space. The placemats dolloped with salsa and cheese. Mortification. Embarrassment. Victor Anthony would be able to read every scrap of meaning in that messy table. How her eagerness to sleep with him overrode every scrap of home training and the habits of a lifetime.

Not what she'd most wanted him to see.

He didn't so much as raise a brow while she bundled away the detritus. Just held their plates until she'd laid out fresh mats for them, then went back for their coffees while she laid out the cutlery.

"So." He paused to bite into the eggs and make yum-noises. "What did you tell everyone to make them flood me with five-star reviews?"

She focused on her plantains. Scraped some salsa onto the forkful with them. She could just envision all her friends turning into heart-eye emojis when they'd read her impulsive, reckless, self-dooming text about Vic and the reviews. They'd spread the love far and wide, too, from what he'd said. For Natalie's mother to be posting positive things about photos of her daughter, favors had for sure been called in.

"I didn't coerce anyone. Whatever they posted was their real thoughts."

"Right. I get that. But before yesterday, I think Serena was the only one to have commented on my work."

"Well, that's just rude of them. They all know social proof is essential for your kind of business."

He traced a finger down her upper arm, which had the irritating effect of lowering her defenses.

She sighed. "Anton mentioned once about you trying to get this best-of designation, and what the site looks for. I didn't think nudging the gals to give you stars would turn into this ...."

"Outpouring of love and support?" Vic smirked.

Gill side-eyed him. "Exactly. It's very over the top of them. I suspect them of texting behind my back about it."

"It wasn't subtle, that's for sure. Again, not that I object. I'm touched you remembered and prodded them to post."

He was so moon-bright, sitting beside her. She could almost make out the waves of contentment and serenity wafting off him. It freaked her out more than anything else about their situation. For decades now, she'd known Vic as a vulcanized ball of energy. Speaking up for himself and Anton when they had a scheme—except in the case of Samster the Hamster, apparently. Getting the boys involved in numerous activities, including finding the right place for Anton to fit in. Flittering from social event to family event to school event and back, always up for the next thing to come along.

And here he was, simply sitting beside her. Not ready to move on, not focused on something around the corner. Just in the moment. It was enough to make her itch to take his pulse.

"What do you have planned for today?" She bit the tender tip of her tongue. If that wasn't a pointed message from her body to her mind, she didn't know what was.

He settled further into his chair and adjusted his coffee cup. "Nothing much. I told Anton I'd clean my room later."

She laughed.

"I know, you don't have to say it. Your folks would be thrilled to know what a good parent to me he is now. Not that he hasn't been keeping me tidy most of my life."

"You're not messy. It's not even high standards with him. Just that everything he has, he has a plan for."

"That, plus his stubborn insistence on giving me a room in his house to start with. He knows I own my own place." It came out almost like a question, but with none of the frustration someone else might feel.

"He knows. It's not for you, I don't think. I think the room is yours because he needs it that way."

Vic snorted. She gathered their plates. He followed her with the cups and poured them each a refill. "But as to the rest of the day, I'm all yours. If you want me. I have a job tonight, but don't need to get set up for that until five-ish."

Every image rushing to fill her sex-sated brain demanded more of him in her bed. She stifled the self-protective impulse to push him out the door, worked with him to clean the kitchen as a nod to their ingrained standards, then led him upstairs and let her body take delicious control of the narrative.

CHAPTER TWENTY-ONE

IT SHOULDN'T MAKE him gulp like a dehydrated dolphin to face Anton after spending hours in his sister's bed.

They'd discussed it.

Not, like, the details of the sex, of course. But the general emotional stuff behind it. The fact he wanted more than anything to earn more mornings eating breakfast with her. All the ways he could imagine Tetris-ing their lives to fit together. How the idea of her made his thoughts drift off into happy-ever-after territory.

So it wasn't some great leap to let Ton know they'd hooked up at last. Besides, the man was a genius. He'd probably clocked Vic's SUV in their drive all night long. It wasn't like they needed to have some in-depth conversation about it.

He knocked on Ton's door, and immediately felt like a cat on the day a cold front swoops into town. Scrambling in circles, leaping from surface to surface, discovering the urgent need to claw under something with not quite enough room for him. The fuck of it was, Ton was the only person for twenty years who never made him feel that way.

"Why didn't you let yourself in?"

"Hell if I know."

Ton squinched his eyes a sec, then shrugged and retreated to the couch. "You know we have the same key?"

Vic joined him. "What?"

"When we bought the place, we rekeyed our doors to match. Seemed easier than having to keep track of each other's keys. This way, we can always let each other in. Always get in to the other's house."

Vic contemplated the info. "Are you telling me this because you let yourself into Gill's in the past few hours?"

Ton snorted. "Not likely."

His inner house-cat wasn't settled down enough for this. "Why then? If you're trying to warn me off your sister or something, just say it flat-out. I can't read between your squeezed-together lines, okay?"

Ton sank further into the cushions, got quieter. Fuck. He hated when Anton retreated almost as much as he hated when he attacked.

"Sorry. I'm a chaos agent today. I shouldn't throw all my mess at you."

They sat staring at the black gloss of the television for a bit. The reflections of his bald dome and of Ton's dark standing shock of hair. He felt the double-thump of the side of Ton's fist against his upper arm: the signal they'd developed as pre-teens to show solidarity, even when they were at odds.

He blew out a longer breath than he'd thought himself capable of and sank into Anton's shoulder. Ton knocked a foot against his in reply.

"Sorry."

"You said that already. Is it because things didn't go well next door? I thought you being there so long was an indication of success."

"No. It was. I ... I'm real happy, Ton."

"Interesting way of showing it."

He huffed. "I know."

Anton's head came to rest on his. "Not interested in

specifics, but if you spent the night, and you're happy, why are you shriveling up on my couch right now?"

"I promised I'd clean my room, remember?"

"Calling it your room is a bigger step than I thought you were ready for."

"I can only fight you Bellamys on so many things at once."

"Hmm." Anton let that sit a bit. "What are you fighting Gill on?"

Everything? Nothing? Vic wondered if he knew the answer. "Far as I can tell, I've got all I could want from her."

"Ew."

"Don't be a baby brother." Vic shoved them both back upright. "I just mean ... we agreed to try it out. We had fun, and plan to spend more time together. She's not afraid anymore that she'll set you off."

Anton went spine-straight. "Set me off?"

"Not in anger."

They sat with that a while, Vic letting Anton's mind process through all the leaps and bounds he always managed. Ton pulled out his phone.

"What are you doing?"

"Texting my sister."

"What? Why?"

"Because now the Bellamys get to fight each other, and you can stay out of it. Go clean your room."

"Ton. Come on." But no matter how he contorted and reached, Anton kept the screen away from him. It was a battle he'd been losing to his taller, longer-armed friend for a decade or more.

Fine, then. He had paying work awaiting him, and a load of laundry to fold. He shoved himself to his feet, and, if only Anton hadn't known him better than he knew himself, he'd have gotten away with lunging for the phone before Ton twisted to standing and escaped out the door.

Goddamn Bellamy family, anyway.

HER DOOR SLAMMED, and Gill jumped half out of her chair.

"Sis, hey, don't let your boyfriend find me." Anton almost danced into her dining room, shoulders shaking.

She wanted to throw something at him. She'd already ignored his taunting texts; he might feel like regressing to their childhood, but she had a slew of papers to grade. "What are you on about?"

He lounged opposite her. "I guess you're playing innocent?"

Damn but she should build more immunity to his playful side. All his fault, of course. If he'd showed it even a tenth as often as a kid, she wouldn't have spent so much time fretting about bringing it out of him. And then his showing up with a grin in her house wouldn't melt her into a sucker-puddle willing to do whatever she could to keep him upbeat.

"Obviously you know Vic spent the night here."

"Obviously." He crossed his arms. "And here it is mid-afternoon. Y'all play Scrabble all morning? Go through some old photo albums? YouTube how to start a podcast?"

"Yep. Got a triple word score for *quizzed.*"

He whistled, mock-impressed.

"Be quiet."

"I will if you will."

She tapped her pen on the table, decisive. "Deal."

Pretending to going back to grading didn't fool him. "I'm happy for y'all."

She grunted. Highlighted a strong topic sentence from one of her most promising students.

"Not just cause he's been hung up on you forever."

"That was puppy stuff."

Now her brother was the one expressing himself nonverbally. She checked out his shift to serious posture. His glare.

"What?"

"Gillian. Are you a hypocrite?"

What? "What nonsense are you talking about?"

"Puppy stuff? Because Vic was, what, just a teenager?"

She closed the laptop. "I mean, yes? Are you suggesting he cultivated some deep and abiding passion for me back then, and has been languishing since until I deigned to notice him?"

"No, you clueless crayon. Kids have kid feelings. Teens have teen feelings. They're valid, but they're also not always the best pattern to build a life around."

Sometimes people complained about the way she spoke. About how she left out logic leaps when she was expressing her thoughts.

Those people never met her brother.

"Aren't we agreeing? Maybe he did crush on me when we were younger, but that doesn't really impact how we're ... together. Now. Now that we're full-ass adults."

Anton kept giving her the 'why aren't you getting this' look.

She sighed.

He sighed. "Gillian. Having a teenage crush doesn't define Vic."

"I know."

"It doesn't mean he couldn't have gone off and fallen in love with anyone else."

In fucking love? No. Not the plan.

Her brother picked up the fear in her face, cause he flicked a spare pen across the table at her. "Or fallen in lust, or dated up a storm, or developed a passionate interest in threesomes. I don't mean he's in love with you, of all people."

"Of all people?" Great. From flustered to offended. Fun emotional pendulum.

Anton huffed. "Calm yourself. I'm spelling out my point here. Which is that you're a hypocrite."

She spun the pen back at him.

"Do you think I don't know how much time you spend big-sistering me? That I never noticed how you're always diving at emotional bullets so I don't have to take them?"

She wouldn't say always. Just as often as she should, being the older sibling. Being the one whose understanding of feelings was more intuitive. Being the empathetic girl-child their parents expected of her. "I only do what's easy for me to make life easier for you."

"I know." He blew out his breath and repeated himself with less agitation in his voice. "I know, Gill. I'm thankful. In case I never said so. Couple of times, all my cartilage would have melted out of me and left me limbless if you hadn't held me solid."

Shit. She flashed onto a few unpleasant childhood afternoons and reached for a napkin to wipe her eyes. "Well. It's just cause I love you. And cause the world is an asshole."

"Truth."

"Okay, then. Good." She tried to act like the discussion was over. Like he could be stopped from laying out his conclusions about her hypocrisy. Because she suspected she knew where he'd go next, and she wasn't quite up for it.

"And even though the world is an asshole, and I'm no good at seeing emotional bullets heading my way, I'm lucky cause I've got you. And also Vic."

Gillian tried to bite down the smile tugging at her cheeks, thinking of times Vic had been the one holding Anton up. Never mind how it proved what a wholly giving and gracious guy he was in general. She didn't need to know all that for the two of them to have some fun in the bedroom.

"And given that I'm slow about recognizing my feelings, and that you know it." His voice had that Very Patient tone he used to explain complex engineering principles to non-science people. "And Vic knows it. And that I was even slower at it when I was a teen. All of that together should be enough for you to under-stand that back when I had a crush on Vic, I was not developing a deep and abiding passion. I took his friendship and the fact I'm gay and threw them into one convenient bucket so I didn't have to carry too much at once. Once I got ahold of another bucket, I sorted it all out so I could keep him but also fall for other guys. I never languished, Gill. I'm not languishing now."

"I know. You have Cisco."

"Even if I never met Cisco. Or Felipe or Otto or Dean, or anyone else. It was puppy stuff, and I never expected Vic to stop crushing on you or any of the other girls he liked. He's super-straight, poor man."

"Poor man." She wiped her eyes again.

"So stop trying to take an emotional bullet no one is shooting, Gillian. Be a full-ass adult, let him be a full-ass adult. And let me be a full-ass adult."

"I am. I always do."

"Do you?" His rebuttal was as fierce as he ever got with her. "Do you get that I can love you both? And your dating doesn't change that? Even if you break up—and even, since this is the worst-case bullet you're trying to get us both to dodge, if you stay together forever."

Instead of waiting the minutes it would likely take for her to formulate a full riposte, he left.

And she was alone.

Just her, and a stack of grading, and an onrush of feelings she was far, far too grumpy to parse.

CHAPTER TWENTY-TWO

THEY BROUGHT dinner to Rachel's. It was so like when Hannah was a newborn and their usual rotation for their monthly meals switched to showing up wherever Rachel and the baby were, so she never had to plan. Or even stand up. Except back then, Rachel was living with her annoying former mother-in-law and one or the other of them would often need to wrestle the baby out of Yia Yia Depy's arms.

Baby Cassandra was a different story. They only had to wrestle her away from each other, and her mother, and her sister. And her father. It was an altogether more genial tussle, enacted while Rachel curled on the sofa and closed her eyes. Gillian took the opportunity to study her most precious friend. Maybe it was that everything under Depy's roof was cast in a dark yellowish tone, while Theo and Rachel's townhome was bright windows and open spaces. Maybe her memories were tinged by her considerable worries about how to help Rachel embark on the life of a single mother. But her heart swelled to see how clear and lax Rach looked in repose. Her keen Mama radar seemed to be churning along on low, rather than vibrating at a constant threat level. More experience with parenting? Cassandra's general chill nature? Or living in a house full of people who loved her, and who she loved to every depth of her self in return?

Probably that love thing.

"Where's your big brain bunked off to?" Natalie held a wine glass out to her.

"Thanks." She sipped the shiraz. "Mmm. Is this to make me forget it's my turn to read Hannah's bedtime story?"

"Stories," Rachel said, without shifting from her cozy curl.

"Even better."

"It's so not your turn," Natalie argued. "You hogged her for practically your whole spring break."

"That doesn't count. We were at my house, so she didn't get to pick her favorites."

"Agree to disagree, woman. Because Serena and I discussed it, and we decided it totally counts."

Serena glanced up from cooing at Cassandra long enough to nod.

"See? So give Hannah-girl her hugs then go make our salad. Probably only use half that jicama—it's a monster."

"I know how to make salad, Natalie."

"Great. Perfect division of labor. I know how to read stories."

"Stop buzzing, y'all." Rachel flapped a hand their way, still without opening her eyes. "Bring me my girl so I can say goodnight."

Gillian gave in, setting aside her wine so she could scoop up Hannah from where she was helping Serena admire her baby sis. Half an hour or so later, it was just the four of them sitting around the table. Cassandra dozed nearby, unbothered by their chatter and the clatter of dinner being served.

"I know she's the most precious baby in a thousand mile radius, but you're gooing all over her an extra amount today," Rachel told Gill.

"She's an extra amount more precious every time I see her is why."

"True that." Rach smiled at her newborn. "Ow, my boobs.

You're supposed to distract me from how sweet she is. I think we're finally past that growth spurt, but no one told my milk ducts yet."

"Poor Rachel."

"Distract or get out."

Serena raised her glass. "Okay, first, a toast to us. It's already been a big year for us, and we're not half through it, but we are rocking it."

They drank to that. "Speaking of the mid-point of the year, do you want to talk wedding at all?"

Rachel slumped against the table with an excess of dramatic gestures. "Gillian. We're celebrating that we survived two weddings already. And me giving birth. And your conference keynote. Can we please not stress me out thinking about how much I have still to do?"

"Okay, okay. If it's better that way for you. We'll just keep waking up to a dozen texts from you every day."

Serena raised her brows. "It was at least twenty yesterday."

"And they started arriving before six a.m.," Nat added.

Rach spared her baby another glance. "Not my fault someone around here isn't clear about how to snooze all night long."

"Do you need me to come over more so you can nap?" Gillian asked, already running through slots in her schedule that would let her spell her friend.

Rachel squeezed her hand. "No. Honest. It's not as easy when Theo's up in Dallas with Andres, of course, but we're getting the hang of everything. As much as we can given Cassandra's growth spurt. Anyway, this is no kind of distraction. Tell me something that's not going to stress me out or make me leak."

"Yeah, Gillian. What can you tell us that will keep Rachel's shirt dry?" Natalie's voice was all tease-song and smug.

"I know what she can tell us." Serena tapped her heart. "I heard a couple of things through the husband grapevine."

Gillian helped herself to more salad, and tried to pass the conversation along with the serving bowl. No one would take it.

She sighed. "First off, your husbands should spend less time gossiping about my life. And B, y'all already know I hooked up with Vic."

None of them looked impressed with her gambit to head off their questions.

"And how up was that hook?" Natalie asked.

"That doesn't even make sense."

"And how many hooks did you up?" Rachel propped her chin on her fist. "Were any of the hooks down low? Did any of the ups get you off the hook?"

"Stop acting like this is a much bigger deal than it is. It's not the first time I've had sex, you know."

Serena toasted her. "That, we know. Wait—what was his name? The one with the teeth?"

"Oh, Jaws!" Nat snorted. "No, he wasn't her first, though. It was that chem major who got mad we only had cow milk."

This was the problem with having friends who'd been around too long. "He name was Jim, not Jaws. And Kaitlynn wasn't mad, just vegan."

"Same thing, in her case." Serena made a thoughtful face. "Do you remember the names of everyone you've been with?"

She nodded like it was natural. "Why, don't you?" She was lying, of course. She'd stopped keeping track, stopped even adding up her numbers, long ago. The tallies didn't matter. What mattered was her autonomy. Her right and privilege to seek pleasure, to give consenting pleasure, where and when she chose.

"She's side-tracking you," Rachel said, then turned her Mama voice on Gillian. "The guys say you and Vic are a couple now. Not just hooking up, not just a one-time. A real honest and true relationship."

She met her friend's stern and slightly pissed off gaze. Nodded.

"And we heard it from them first, why exactly?"

Gillian found herself staring at her dessert fork, willing the baby to wake up and take the focus off her. Which was more than jelly-spined enough to jolt her into truth telling. She sighed. "Vic is ... y'all, he's so soft. I can't even gratify Natalie with a pun about it. He's always had this, you know, shell about him. Like he's unbreakable, tough no matter what. Rolls in anywhere and is at total ease, everyone's pal."

"He's affable, I get that," Serena said.

"It's not just that. I mean, he genuinely is a people person. Otherwise he'd never have his job, I don't think. But I'm talking about what's underneath."

Nat smirked and everyone shushed her before she could make jokes.

"Is it bad, the softness? Why is it bad, I mean?" Rachel asked.

"No. Not bad. But I can't ignore it. Can't just go to bed with him and have him talk about his heart and how he wants to be a couple and let him bring me coffee while I grade and just ... not know all the time that his shell might break."

"Raise your hand if you're remembering a time Gillian told you to not borrow trouble," Nat said to the others. All their hands shot towards the ceiling.

"Before I met Theo's parents and sisters, she told me if they turned out to be possum-suited suffocators, we'd deal with them one claw at a time. And I shouldn't spent the whole drive to Austin turning them into Depy in my imagination."

"See? Rachel's right." Natalie slid the wine bottle her way, which gave Gill an excuse to look away while she listened to her friends pile on. "You're turning him into a problem before you even take the time to know if dating him means you might like his soft side."

"It's not my liking the soft side I'm worried about." Her breastbone felt inadequate to the task of keeping her most vital organ in place.

"Well, then, what is, hon?" Rachel's gentleness pierced all her meagre defenses.

She blurted the words before giving herself a chance to coat them in ironic distance. "What if I break his shell and all that softness spills out and solidifies and then I've changed him forever and he can't rein it in and every time I need soft he's all hard and rubbery and every time I act sharp he's got no armor I can bounce off and every time I look for the Vic I've known all my life, the one who gets all my stuff because he saw me grow up in my family, he's gone and this mess of goop is all I can have?"

As distractions for Rachel went, it worked just fine. But none of their comforting, no answers to their questions, and no amount of shiraz quelled the worries buzzing through her brain.

CHAPTER TWENTY-THREE

TON NUDGED his shoulder into Vic, almost causing him to fumble his grip on the controller and miss a jump. "She's back," he said. But they'd gamed together for decades, and Vic was wise to Ton's tricks.

He didn't bother to respond. He wasn't going to lose this round, and there was a tricky sequence coming up.

"You may as well jump into the lava now. You know you're not gonna get through this before she stops in for you."

He nudged Ton back. "I didn't come here for her. It's not like I'm gonna stop hanging with you because of her. And anyway, it's her girls night."

"I know what night it is. And you know she stops by here when she's back to give me the gossip."

Okay, yes, it wasn't the first time he'd been planted on Ton's sofa when Gillian's monthly dinner with her friends concluded and she smushed in beside her brother. She pretty much ignored him all those times, so no reason he should expect her to reach out to him tonight.

Seconds later, her feet sounded on the porch, followed by her key in the lock. "Hey."

Some kind of ingrained response to her voice had him whipping around to smile at her. Next thing he knew, Ton was laughing and the console was bleeping to him about his descent into the lava pit of death.

Great.

He didn't dignify the loss with a response. He slid his controller onto the coffee table and ignored Ton's gloating avatar taking a victory lap.

"Having fun?" she asked. And unlike every other time she came into Ton's half of the duplex, Gill squeezed in beside him. Between her hand on his thigh and her kiss to his cheek, his defeat in the game didn't sting much after all.

IT WASN'T hard to lure Vic to join her on her side of the wall. She headed over first to straighten herself out while her brother and Vic went through their farewell routines. Some ex of Anton's once said it was odd that someone as taciturn as Anton had so much to say to Victor. Just went to prove he wasn't the right guy for her brother, since Anton talked plenty—or some version of plenty—to those he valued. Sure, the list wasn't often longer than her and Vic, but it didn't stop it being true.

By the time Vic let himself into her house, Gill was back to fussing at her nerves. Her friends' assurances aside, she knew she and Vic being together risked changing his connection to her family.

Or maybe her fear stemmed from somewhere else. Like her life-long definition of herself as Anton's sister. And protector, and translator, and friend. If she took Vic away from him, no matter how much she never intended to do any such thing, she would break so many of those self-appointed roles. And that? That would break her.

But Vic showed up with a gleam in his eye and mint on his breath and no shoes, since he apparently left them in her brother's hallway. And who was she, she asked her brain gremlins, to argue with a barefoot Vic? She led him up to her bedroom and switched her appraisal from his gentle eyes to the torso he bared as he crossed the threshold.

She was for sure unable to argue with a shirtless Vic.

He bracketed his hands on her waist and said, "I wasn't waiting for you."

"Never said you were."

"I went to Ton's cause I always go to Ton's if he's in town and I don't have a gig."

"Noted. Which is all facts I knew from long ago."

He flexed his fingers into the flesh between her hips and ribs, letting out a low growl. "Sass suits you. Makes me even hotter for you."

Well, hell if she was arguing with a sex-smitten Vic. She scraped her nails along his scalp and pulled his mouth to hers. His beard growth scraped her cheek and chin as he nipped his way down her pulse line to the tender hollow of her neck.

"Fuck," he groaned.

She gyrated her hips, and his swearing got more vehement. She backed them to her bed and they landed with Vic on his side, hand shoving his jeans down while she tugged off their shirts. They were getting downright efficient at stripping each other.

And she was far from accustomed to the sight of Victor Anthony, nude, flushed with passion, looking at her like he'd won a prize.

Or to the feel of his warm, calloused fingers tracing up her spine and cradling her nape.

Or to his taste. His tongue and lips, firm and gentle and tender and demanding. His fresh exhales and the ravenous way he inhaled her own breaths. How he hummed when her tongue twisted with his, and how his whole body was an extension of their kiss—flexing and teasing and rubbing as his devouring mouth explored hers.

His kiss stole her fucking soul.

She broke away to shove their clothes and her blankets to the floor. "I should gag you. You're distracting me."

Damn smug eyes. "I think I'll decline, thank you."

"So polite. How about a blindfold?"

"How about you tie me to the headboard, but you wear the blindfold?"

His voice was teasing, but she hovered over him, considering it. "Huh. Interesting. Why?"

"Well, the tying because I like it when you control the pace. I like knowing you can use me to get the depth and the motion you need to get yourself off. And the blindfold because every time we fuck, I get lost in your gorgeous eyes. It'll free me up to stare at how your body takes from mine, and the way you'll maybe have to use your hands on yourself cause mine are up here." He patted the headboard twice.

Gill collapsed onto him. "You are such a toad-monger. Now I don't have a choice, and it's not like I've got handcuffs here."

"No? Any scarves?"

"We live in Houston; my scarf stash isn't so vast."

"I can run next door and raid Ton's closet for some ties." He made to get up.

She shoved him back. "Shush. You can not. I need you on this bed." Her damn clit was aching already.

"As the lady demands."

"Oh, you listen to demands? Fine, then. You just hold on to the headboard without restraints, and I'll put on my sleep mask. But the second I feel your hands on me, I'm taking it off."

Vic scooted up and anchored himself against a couple of pillows. "Deal."

Before he lost access to his hands, he wrapped a leg around hers and urged her close for another kiss. She wasn't about to fight him on it, not when the position let her rock her pelvis into the muscled contours of his thigh. Each second she aimed to quench her thirst for him, it only grew. Finally she took his hands in hers and guided them to the spindles behind him.

His eyes burned at her, and she fought the impulse to turn off the light. Instead, she grabbed her mask and a condom, securing the second before she donned the first. The mask didn't block all light, but it stopped her from seeing anything but a glow at the edges. She closed her eyes to steady herself, and in an instant, her senses transitioned. Vic's indrawn hiss whip-cracked at her. The air played cool and naughty tricks on her tight nipples. Their mingled arousal was the most potent aroma in the room.

Slowly, she reached for him. Her palms flattened on his abdomen, and she drew them higher, to the valley made by his pecs. His bunched shoulders and the soft furze at his armpits exposed while he maintained his overhead grip. The bumps of his ribs down his sides and the gentle glide of flesh veeing towards his pelvis.

Another gasp. "Gillian."

"Victor." Was her voice always so full, so fervent? She straddled him.

"If I suggest this again, remind me how I'm a frog-monger."

"Toad-monger." She bit her lip with desire, and with joy, because rickety as the blindfold made her feel, his voice stabilized everything. She used his cock to tease her clit, dragging it through her folds and pleasuring her aroused bud with the hard shaft in her hand.

"Really want to grab your tits right now. Or your hips."

"Hmm." She wasn't quite ignoring him, but she was having plenty of fun doing things her way.

"Gill." Somehow he pulsed harder, and she could tell from the changing pressure behind her that he'd braced his feet on the mattress. He used the leverage for an insistent pelvic thrust. It caught her just right, a solid slide along her labia, and she couldn't put either of them off any longer.

Everything in her was over-sensitized. She couldn't tell through the buzzing in her ears if it was her groan or his that filled the room as she lowered herself onto his shaft. She could practically trace the course of the air filling her lungs and spreading through her body. The rush of blood making her head light and her sheath heavy with need. Each inch of him filling her, each contraction squeezing him. She tightened her thighs to his hips and arched back, giving herself the balance she needed so urgently to free her hands to race over her own torso. She cupped her breast, pinching her nipple between her fingers, and scraped the other hand down his flexing abdomen on her way to her clit.

"Fucking fucking yes. Gill. Those little circles, rub like that for me. I can see you getting wetter. Smell you."

Feel her, too, she bet, from the way his words and her hands had her clenching that much harder around his cock. She sucked her fingers and moved to her other nipple, but never let up on her clit. Just varied the pressure some, in time to his withdrawals and the rise and fall of her hips. Arched back a touch more, just enough so his shaft rubbed harder against her inner walls, and then she was done. No more control. Folded her body over his, reaching for his head so she could plaster kisses on him while she shuddered and flew and her other hand pressed tight on her clit and she came all over him. All around him. And he ripped her mask away and grabbed tight to her ass and thrust and fucked up into her, his lips all over kisses and her name and kisses and curses and teeth nipping her shoulder and her name and his breath and her name.

CHAPTER TWENTY-FOUR

I**T WAS** the time of year when he traded his monthly calendar for a weekly one. And resorted to color-coding to keep everything straight. At least he'd managed to figure out automation of a lot of the accounting stuff since the prior summer, which saved him a good few hours every week.

He wanted to spend every one of those saved hours in Gillian's bed.

The multicolored scrawls all over his calendars boded well for his business, but not for his growing infatuation with having her body pressed to his. And the closer they got to summer, the more intense her own work got. She was always coming up on the deadline to submit her syllabus for online summer classes, or getting another sheaf of stuff to mark, or proctoring finals.

So when Ton called to invite him camping, he said no before he even moved to his desk to check.

"You sure? Gill said she thought y'all were free."

"She did?" His heart was doing silly things again at this evidence of her wanting to spend any time with him. Even if that time was in a tent.

He never had taken to camping the way the rest of the Bellamy family did. Went along with them plenty, especially once they'd gotten a two-man tent that he and Ton could pitch on their own. Those campfire nights were the ones when the four Bellamys were most in accord, and maybe that's why they were also the ones where he felt most like an outsider trying to edge his way into their circle of warmth and stability.

"She said you had the one night open, anyway. Didn't know if that meant you could spare the time to drive out to Enchanted Rock, though."

He checked the relevant days. "Let me make a couple of calls. When do you need to know?" Anton phoning him instead of texting was code for his friend's anxiety to settle everything.

"I need to tell Cisco if it's on or not. If not, he's going to help someone with a dude ranch that weekend. But he'd rather camp with us."

"No doubt." Cisco was full of tales about the guests at dude ranch vacations. Plenty of lovely people mixed in with the arrogant and entitled folks. They were the ones that made for the best stories. It was good side gig money, but not his favorite way to spend time.

"So let me know in forty-seven minutes."

He laughed, like Ton knew he would. Their high school classes had run forty-seven minutes, and whenever they didn't have a period together they'd meet up between classes to get on with whatever conversation occupied them at the moment. Usually Vic was the one talking. He was the one with all the goings on—theatre and soccer and yearbook and whatever else—while Ton was the quiet, calm epicenter of his whirlwind. "Kay-o. Call you later."

After hanging up, he spun a couple of twirls in his desk chair, looking for focus. His calendar. Right. He was checking his calendar. Because his best friend wanted him to join him camping. Wanted him to be in the circle of chairs around the fire, an integral part of the experience.

And, also, so did his girlfriend. He couldn't guess if she wanted to call him boyfriend or not, but Vic was planting his flag. He knew what she was to him. He knew what he wanted to be to her.

———————

DID she know how she ended up in the back seat of Anton's truck, squeezed knees to thighs against Vic for a solid four hours of freeway time?

Not entirely. Not in a way she could name without first having to face her skittering, subterranean, skin-prickling feelings.

After a pit stop at Bucee's—Cisco insisted on visiting the miraculous joy of the truck stop/convenience store/land of ultra-clean restrooms and a dozen flavors of kolaches—Vic asked her to hold his coffee so he could slip into the rear seat ahead of her. As she climbed up to join him, he twisted so his legs stretched into her space. "Now you do the same and we'll have a little more room."

"Hmm." She didn't try to suppress the skepticism in her throat. Not that he was wrong about the limb Jenga option. Just that ... well, thing was, never mind this couples camping trip they'd somehow ended up on, so far she and Vic hadn't really been An Item in front of her brother.

He knew. Obviously. He wasn't acting like it mattered. Like they were anything but his sister and his best friend just hanging out, almost like normal except for how she and Vic fucked now.

She pushed her musings away. "Tell me again why we didn't bring your SUV for this drive? Or take two cars?"

Anton snorted. "Vic would never let his precious vehicle get covered with country dirt."

Vic landed a soft blow to the back of Anton's headrest. "You know what a pain it is to vacuum out all that dust before I lay my equipment down there? I'm not into hauling a bunch of mud-caked tent poles rolling everywhere when I have that Lawson event on Friday."

"Such a diva."

Cisco huffed a laugh. Anton flicked him a look she interpreted as, "Don't say it."

He did, though. "You can talk."

Anton's fingers flexed on the steering wheel. Vic and Gill caught each other's looks. Turned out their intertwined legs weren't so tense-making after all. Instead, the contact heightened their shared non-verbal amusement at her brother's expense.

"Stop smirking at me."

She filled her tone with sisterly concern. "Who, me?"

"Both of you. You think this rearview only shows I-10 rolling out behind us?"

Vic tilted his head, faux-serious. "Oh, please. Explain the geometry of mirrors for us, Ton. Or is it physics? Geology? Astronomy?"

"Fuck you."

Cisco's shoulders shook so hard he had to set down his bag of Beaver Nuggets to gain control of himself. His mirth prompted Anton to bark a quick laugh, and Gill gave Cisco one more check in the pro column. He'd been raking up the points with her lately. But much as this trek out to E-Rock was the first time she and Vic would share a tent with Anton around, it was also the longest time either of them had spent with her brother and Cisco as a couple.

Probably something she needed, if she was going to banish those vestiges of her hang-ups about Anton having feelings for Victor. She knew he was right—they were both right—that the stress and guilt she'd taken on about sleeping with Vic were no longer relevant.

Even if she would never tell either Vic or Anton about the way her brother's face fell that time he saw Vic coming out of her bedroom. It was a decade ago, and Vic didn't see, and Anton maybe couldn't have guessed what emotions his face had conveyed.

No need for her to hold on to it, since they weren't.

So pure logic dictated that she should shelve her outsized thoughts and too-tight nerves and find a way to regard this trip as a chance for them all to relax into getting along as a foursome.

They'd booked one of the remote campsites, which meant hiking a few miles up from the parking lot with all their gear and water and food. Cisco stopped griping about it once they'd trekked passed the easy camping area near the entrance with all the family groups, and were immersed in the solitude of the trees and rocks and vistas. He and Vic took over unpacking the gear while she and her brother got into the full swing of set up.

"Where are my pegs?" Anton griped at her.

"Up your butt," she said automatically. Cisco exploded into a coughing fit that had her rethinking her words. Anton covered his eyes with his hands.

Vic shook his head. "You know, it's okay to come up with all new inside jokes that aren't full of inappropriate sex references."

"We didn't know what it meant."

"The first few times, sure." He turned to Cisco. "But then I'm at home after one trip, doing my usual magpie chatter at my parents cause I hadn't learned how they didn't pay much attention to anything I said, and I mention how these two always say that about the tent pegs and my dad actually has me repeat myself. So I looked it up. Picture me at thirteen, stumbling across a little more information than I expected, and then having to tell Ton and Gillian about it."

Cisco fell into another coughing fit so intense that Anton went to grab him a drink from the cooler. He muttered something about the three of them being joined at the psychic hip, but probably he meant it in a good-natured way. Never mind how it somehow made her feel like an outsider to their camaraderie. Or maybe how she suddenly felt like an outsider to the Vic she'd thought she'd known.

For the rest of the evening, while she and Anton moved through their comfortable routine of arranging their gear, dealing with the troublesome cook stove neither of them ever got round to replacing, and rock-paper-scissoring for who got first crack at the wash water, Vic played tour guide to the Bellamy siblings at a campsite.

He kept them all laughing, but oh, she squirmed. Every time he said something like that bit about using magpie chatter to get his folks' attention, or explained to Cisco that no, he never bothered to let home know where he and Anton had been when they decided to go camp on the banks of the Brazos during what turned out to be a fifteen-year-flood, or made casual reference to how her parents always packed extra mandarin oranges because he devoured them.

It was everything she already knew about his life and his interactions with her family, but nothing she'd framed from his perspective before.

CHAPTER TWENTY-FIVE

CIRCLED around the cold cookstove with the lanterns on low and the crickets making a racket, he expected to have hit that point where the discomfort of dirt and rocks and the whims of the weather faded, and campfire camaraderie kicked in. And far as things with Ton and Cisco went, he was there. The three of them had plenty to say—or he and Cisco had plenty to say, with Ton between them comfortable chiming in or just listening as suited him.

It was the other mostly silent Bellamy he wasn't sure about. By the time they crawled into their tent, it had been maybe a full hour since she'd expressed one of her opinions.

"You doing okay?"

The lantern wasn't any better at letting him read her face than it had been when they were under the stars. "Sure."

"Not sure I buy that."

She rolled to face him, which helped. "I didn't think to pack any mandarins."

He laughed a little. "We all had access to the packing list. If I'd wanted them, I'd have added them. Or packed them myself."

"Still." Her furrowed brow wasn't making her mood any clearer. "I remembered the Granny Smiths for Anton."

"Gillian. It's not your job to pack our favorite snacks. You're not our mom."

She shifted. Her restless legs shushed against their nylon sleeping bag. "All those times you camped with us, that was you needing someone to take care of you."

He closed his eyes. Even the crickets couldn't soothe his flash of irritation. "I'm not Oliver Twist. Yeah, there were lots of ways being with y'all was more of a traditional family experience, but it's not like my parents didn't provide for me. Or like yours were …."

"Mine were what?" Her face was calm, but her voice had an edge.

"Perfect. I was going to say 'perfect,' but that's not even the thing. We both know none of us would call them ideal. You're certainly not who you are because you followed the path they set out for you."

Her legs shushed again as she balled up her body. "At least they went to your plays."

"And provided me with fruit, I know. Anything on the stereotype of fifties parenting I needed, I got from them. I don't deny that. Look, I love your parents. They made a difference to me, growing up. It's no secret I'm all in on you Bellamys."

"That's right. Us Bellamys."

"What's that supposed to mean?"

"We've been taking care of you since you and Anton met. And I'm not suggesting it's not mutual with you and him. God knows how he'd face the world sometimes if not for you."

"Hey, give him credit. I can't get why you act like he's still eleven."

"Yes, fine, I know. He deserves more. But there you go again —we're in the middle of talking about us, and he's in the mix."

"I didn't bring him up."

"You didn't have to. He's always there. And don't twist that to mean I mind—he's my brother. He was my brother before he was your twin."

Well, that had bite. He scrubbed his eyes and worked on keeping his voice quiet enough to not drift to the next tent over. "I don't follow what you're saying now. I feel like everything's coming out at once and, news flash: I was never enmeshed enough in your family to track the leaps y'all sometimes make. You want to bring me oranges when I never asked that of you, same time as you want me to praise your parents' ideals when you work so hard to forge a path different from them."

The lantern flickered and dimmed further, which probably counted as some kind of cosmic message instead of a need to buy new batteries. He switched it off and sank to the ground beside Gill.

She drew in a deep breath and unfurled herself. "I know all about my parents' flaws. Believe me. And I shouldn't have given in to that tug to be the caretaker."

He slid a hand over enough to link his fingers with hers. She didn't pull away. "It's okay to care about making the trip good for each other."

"Yeah." She squeezed his hand. "Yeah, you're right. And I know we already talked this out, but tonight I heard you tell stories about all these ways you've anchored yourself to us. Turned to us for stability when your family was in the wind. But right now, I feel like Anton is your Scylla, and I'm Charybdis drowning in my own whirlpool, and you're the one who has to navigate between us. And maybe you should just steer towards Anton's shore, because you know you'll be safe there. Leave me to my whirlpool."

Now he had to brush up on Greek mythology to be taken seriously by her? "Gillian. I'm not picking between you two. I already picked him, years ago, but that doesn't mean I can't chose you, too. Not because you're good at buying fruit, or because you know all the inside jokes about the great outdoors. Because you're you."

By the time Anton and Cisco made it back from climbing, she and Vic had done their hike up the pink granite mound of Enchanted Rock and basked in the miles of mesquite plains and rocky outcrops stretching in every direction around them. He'd carried one of his lighter cameras—no pile of lens attachments and light monitors or whatever all that stuff he used was. She'd carried the water bottles and day bag.

Between them they'd settled into a pace, walking uphill, that took on a form of communion between them. The way they passed the water back and forth. The way she paused when he was taking shots. And he paused when he outpaced her up up particularly steep section of the trail. Not that she had trouble with climbing. All those mornings on the elliptical conditioned her for more stamina than she remembered from the last time she climbed E-Rock. But her brain was wrestling with her heart, and with everything that made her jump into what Vic would call overprotective sister mode. What Anton called her being a pain in his ass.

She didn't know what Cisco would call it, just that some looks between them had her suspecting that she was the odd one out among these three men. She didn't like it. She didn't want anyone making allowances for her, or excusing her for being emotional, or approaching her with gentleness as she processed her feelings. She could for sure deal without any of that bullshit in her life.

So while she worked on shoving those thoughts away, her footing was not as secure as she might like. Not that she explained one ounce of herself to Vic as he braced with one foot uphill, ready to reach out a hand if she needed it. Maybe she didn't need to. Maybe that's what this unspoken transfer of water bottles and chin nods towards a particularly cute kid rumble-stumbling along the rocks was all about. What did she know from how relationships worked? Only time she dated anybody this long it was a colleague already under contract to move to Montana for the next academic year.

So, probably she and Vic were fine.

Probably she and Anton were fine, too. He and Cisco seemed chill enough while they were reliving every belay and foothold of their adventure up the rock face. No one snarked while they loaded up the truck, or rolled their eyes at her for her one last trip to the restroom before they headed out.

Rolling into the outskirts of Austin, she nudged Vic with her knee. "Stay for dinner with me tonight?"

He glanced at his phone. Like they were unaware of the exact time Anton predicted their arrival at the duplex. She'd given up on teasing her brother about his ETAs, since he was always right, no matter what the GPS predicted.

"Ah, yeah, Sure. That works." Vic nodded decisively. Like there was nothing hesitant about him.

"Count us out," Anton offered from behind the wheel. "Cisco's sister made enchiladas."

He shook his head and drawled, "Only if we get there in time. They go fast."

"Oh, we'll get there in time. Hundred fifty-two minutes to my door. Seventeen to unload and put on a fresh shirt. Eleven minutes to your sister's place."

Cisco's response was muttered head shaking.

"Don't doubt him," Vic said. "He'll gloat when he proves you wrong."

"It's not doubt I'm feeling. Trust," Cisco said, which made Anton take a hand off the steering wheel to cup Cisco's cheek.

And if that didn't prove what an asshole she was, Gillian didn't know what did.

Vic glanced to her like he was checking in on what she was thinking. She grinned back as if to say, "See, everything's happy. No issues, no stress." And if the silence and slightly inane conversation that buoyed them all over the next hundred and fifty minutes was any indication, she was almost entirely clear. No one would call her out, and that meant the past was past and they could stay focused on the now.

CHAPTER TWENTY-SIX

JUNE ROLLED in and she and Vic had what almost seemed like an easy routine. Her job became less intense while his grew more consuming, but they fit each other into the space they had.

"Are you okay with stopping by mine? I need to switch out my battery packs."

She handed him the last equipment case to load into his admittedly pristine cargo space and smiled. "Sure, no problem. I've got my bag so we can sleep there if you like."

She'd packed a change of clothes for the day's festivities, in case she needed to get tidy after they'd all been paddling. Rachel and Theo had rented a bunch of single and double kayaks at Buffalo Bayou Park, where they'd had their first date. Everyone hung out on the water for an hour, racing each other, splashing, and showing off, before heading to the restaurant above the rental shop for a charming meal on the patio overlooking the bayou. As pre-wedding parties went, it wasn't exactly wild, but they'd been surrounded by trees and sun and water. Also a few egrets and cranes and ducks delighting the kids from where they hung out on the banks with Theo's ex-wife and her husband. And the restaurant was beguiling mixture of relaxed and elegant that personified Theo and Rachel's relationship.

At lunch, people huddled around Vic while he previewed the pics he'd taken from the water. He scrolled past an embarrassing number of shots of her turning to look at him over her shoulder in their double kayak. Since he'd been working, she'd done most of the paddling, meaning they'd not traveled quite as effortlessly as some of the other duos on the water. And she'd glared at him every time he teased her about it. Now she suspected he'd mostly done it to get her to turn around so he could catch her with his camera. It was perverse of her to be charmed by that, but apparently endorphins had as much of an effect on her as they did on all of her friends when they'd been getting into their relationships.

And if that didn't give her pause, here on the brink of her third wedding in seven months. She was not going to turn into a besotted princess just because she and Vic had great sex.

He hopped in the SUV beside her and gave her a look. "You okay?"

She pulled her cloak of coolness around herself. "Of course. Got everything?"

"Yep." And they set off.

As he took the exit towards his house she noticed the apartment complex and large grocery store on the feeder road. "Those are new."

He glanced. "About three or four years, I guess."

Had it been that long since she was in their old neighborhood? He navigated streets that were at once familiar and disorienting, with the occasional large brick house filling every foot of lots that used to hold small ranch homes. Signs of prosperity and modernity that didn't quite fit with her remembrance of a solidly middle class neighborhood. "I don't know why I expected nothing around here would change."

He glanced at her. "Hope you're not too disappointed by my house."

"Why, what did you do do it, turn it into a four story glass and brick behemoth?"

He huffed. "No. Nothing so ambitious. Just aimed to make it mine."

She'd been to his house before. Back when she could first drive and the boys couldn't, there must have been a thousand trips to drop off or pick up Anton, to fetch them from theatre rehearsal and deliver Vic home, to run Anton back to Vic's house because he'd forgotten something there. She'd pulled into the same driveway, stood at the same front door. She'd never hung out the way Anton had, but Vic's parents would invite her in if it was taking a while to rouse the boys from whatever world they'd disappeared into. So she recognized some differences right away. How he'd opened up the entry into the living room. How everything was now blues and silvers instead of browns and greens.

She said nice things as he let her back and poured them drinks.

He gestured her into one the chairs around his kitchen table, and joined her. "This is weird."

"What's weird? That you still live in your parents' house? Lots of people do that."

He waved that aside. "I bought it ten years ago."

That long ago? "You were still a teenager."

"Well, they wanted to go. We made a deal with my college fund."

Her brow furrowed. "What did you do to pay for college then?"

He shrugged. "Scholarships. Gigs. Took photos for half the senior class."

Right. Far be it from her to pass judgment on the way his family worked. "So what's weird then?"

He eyed her over the rim of his glass. Seemed like he was waiting for her to wade through her own mystification and answer her own question. Finally, he said, "It's been weeks now with you and me, right? Months. And this is the first time you've come here."

Well, *fuck*. Was that weird? It was weird, right? But he always saw her at her place. Because he was always coming over to hang with Anton. So it just made sense that when it turned into them having sex they'd keep doing it at hers. He'd never asked her over, and she wouldn't have objected. They'd just gotten into a rhythm she was only now learning might not work for him.

She eyed him. "Am I supposed to have asked to come over?"

"No." He sighed, and repeated more gently, "No, that's not what I mean. But I was struck when you talked about the way the neighborhood changed. All these things are background to me now. I don't even notice them. And you haven't been here in so long that it took you by surprise."

"Sorry," she tried, not sure if that was the right response. Not sure what he was looking for from her.

"No, that's not what I mean. I just think it's not something we've talked about."

"What isn't?"

"That I'm always the one to come to you."

"Hang on." She nudged her glass aside. "It sounds like you're mad. Are you mad?"

"I'm not, I swear."

"So, what then?"

He ran his hand over his smooth-shaved scalp. "I'm not saying there's anything wrong, exactly. I don't know. Maybe this doesn't make any sense. It's just somehow a little weird to see you in my place. And it's a little weird to realize that this is the first time it's ever happened."

Her mind was leapfrogging around to put his questions in a context she could understand. Something that made sense of his unease but didn't force her into a mea culpa she didn't feel.

"I ... admit it's strange to realize we haven't been here together. And I'm glad you spoke up about it bothering you. We'll make a point of being more equitable about our locations from now on, yeah?"

He waited her out a bit longer than she expected, but smiled when she said, "So now we get to break in your bed, right?"

Because maybe they were on shaky ground, maybe not. But she figured there was one tried and true way to put him in accord with her. She grabbed her bag and lured him to his bedroom. It was obviously once his parents' room, but everything about it now seemed like Vic: bookcase full of photography manuals and equipment, gorgeously framed nature images, modern king-sized bed with a dappled teal and gray spread.

It was all perfectly nice and entirely comfortable. No reason at all for her to feel like a porcupine far from the confines of her den.

HE FELT like he was giving in, but without ever defining what concessions he was granting. What had he wanted? Her to know she'd taken his going to her place for granted. What had she said? That she heard him and would course-correct.

So there was no problem with drawing her onto his mattress and letting their hands carry them both away. And it eased an ache inside him, to see her in this space he'd created. To prop her on his pillows as they kissed. To reach into his own bedside table for the condom.

It was reflexive now, the way his body reacted to her nearness. The ratcheting of tension down his spine when they kissed. The rush of his blood at the scent of her arousal. They didn't always have to talk during sex. They could communicate with touches and eye contact and their sighs when he entered her.

And maybe not every time had to elevate them to the clouds. Sometimes sex was a great release without also being a stitch in the pattern drawing them closer.

So there was no problem with that, either. He'd wanted her in his home, and in his bed. All that had happened. He hadn't conceded anything, and neither had she, and that was ... fine.

CHAPTER TWENTY-SEVEN

"THERE NOW, I hope that proves I've got no problem coming to you." She actually giggled at her own joke, which was certainly a choice.

Not one that he would have made in his present mood.

"Vic?" she asked, propping up on an elbow to run her eyes all over his face.

He offered up a smile.

"Wait, seriously, is this a thing? Do we need to get all couples counseling about it?"

"Is that your way of admitting that we're an actual couple?"

"What are you talking about? Of course we're a couple. Or didn't you notice that we just did some super fun sex things?"

"Not like that's a precious commodity to be gotten from you."

"Excuse me, are you actually shaming me right now?"

"God no, of course not. You know your sex life is your own business."

"Okay, yes, I do know that, but you're the one who just brought it up like our intimacy means nothing."

"That's not what I meant. Of course, it means something. To me, it means everything. But ...."

"But what?"

He couldn't keep looking at her uncomprehending face. Either she didn't get him at all, or she was great at pretending. "But you never want to hear what it means to me. You don't want to think in terms of you and me. You don't want to rearrange your life in a significant way, just because of me."

"I don't? What am I doing here then?"

Her students must quake in fear of being the reason for that sharp voice. But her power over him wasn't that of a teacher over a student, and he didn't need to flinch from her scorn. "Showing up with one single change of clothes so you have an excuse get out of here as soon as possible, as far as I can tell."

"That's fantasy on your part. I'm doing no such thing."

"No? What's your plan for now, then? Want to hang out, watch a movie with me? Chat about what we'll do the rest of the weekend? Or next week? Next month?"

She snarked right back at him. "I mean, I've got a summer term lecture to record. Paper conferences to give. A letter of recommendation to write. It's my job. I can't really ignore all that."

"Was I asking you to ignore it?"

"No. I don't know what you're asking."

"Nothing. I'm not asking anything. I never ask anything. I take what I get. Whatever attention you have for me, whatever time you have for me. That's all I need. Definitely no indication that you care about me beyond this." He sank into the bedding, hoping she didn't notice the chills crawling up and down his limbs.

"Okay, let me get this straight. What all of your mumbling asides and nonspecific jabs add up to is, you want to find out about commitment. That's what you want to talk about."

He flinched away from the darts in her voice. And in some ways from her words themselves. "Is that what you think?" Of course that was what she thought. She was the great Gillian Bellamy, master thinker. So if she thought it, it must be true.

His jaw clenched as he wrestled with the fact that of course she was right. His griping aside, his heart kind of lurched when she'd said 'commitment.' Not from any uncertainty about his feelings. He wanted her. He wanted her to want him, even though she'd never said a thing about any lasting affection between them. Even though she always talked about that day, the next day, the next week, but never anything further. Even though he'd been in her world more than long enough to understand that she did not do long term relationships.

It was still what he wanted.

And seriously, fuck his life because no way could he figure out how to ask anything of this sort from her. Not because he feared her not wanting the same thing. He had reason to hope she might get there, eventually. But because all along she'd been right: losing her would change his relationship to Anton. If he screwed up—like he'd screwed up other friendships and relationships, like he screwed up being a son whose family cared to stick around—his one true anchor could go sinking away from him. And if he was going to lose Gillian, his need for Anton would be nine thousand times stronger.

———————————

VIC TRIED TURNING the subject aside. "It's fine. I'm just raw right now; we don't have to get into it. Maybe we should order some dinner? How about that mac and cheese place?"

But she hadn't made tenure track because she was easy to distract, or afraid to tackle tough subjects. He wanted to talk about it, they'd talk about it. "First off, if it's bothering you we shouldn't put it off," she started. His shoulders punching into the pillows reminded her that Vic wasn't a wayward student she had to bring to task.

"I guess me being raw doesn't matter, then. Look, you're going to say you told me so, but I'm tense about losing Anton.

On top of everything else. So maybe I should sort that out before we talk more."

Maybe she was raw, too, because her words rushed out at him. "Anton? But—I thought we'd sorted that. No matter what happens with you and me, nothing will change with you and Anton. I'm not gonna break his heart by demanding that he never see his best friend again."

"So you're just gonna break mine."

"I mean, obviously, that's not my goal. I like what we're doing. I'm having fun with you."

"Fun."

Never had a word sounded so flat and uninviting. She could write a paper on intonation and intent that would blow even Fred out of the water.

"Well, that comforts me."

"No, come on, Vic. I'm just saying. You're acting like we have to re-litigate this whole thing over my brother. And what I'm saying is, we don't. We're fine. He's fine. You saw him with Cisco; you know he doesn't need us to baby him."

"Oh, I noticed that, did I? I'm the one who's finally learned that him having a crush on me when we were teenagers is nothing compared to decades of solid friendship?"

"Well, look at you arguing the irrelevance of teenage crushes."

"Fucksake, Gillian. Yeah, I got off on thinking about you when I was a kid. Yeah, we had a hot night together ten years ago. Those things don't signify—to use one of your favorite words—compared to our actual adult relationship here. Don't you think we'd be interested in being together if we hadn't known each other for so long?"

She caught air in her esophagus, startled to contemplate the idea. "I don't know."

"What do you mean you don't know? You don't think I'd want to fall in love with someone who's brilliant and beautiful and witty and laser-focused on her life? Like it's important, like it's vital. You don't think I'd want someone who might turn one-sixteenth of that intensity on me? Someone who cares about me as deeply as she cares about everything else? Someone who might someday act like keeping me around is as important to her as it is to me?"

His questions threw her into a tailspin. After all that he said, only one thing was glaring at her. Like, flashlight straight to the eyeballs in the middle of the night glare. "In *love?*"

"Yes, Gillian, I'm in love with you. That can't be news. Unless you're nine hundred times more oblivious than I think you are."

"But we never ... I never."

"Never, never, never. I got it. It's fine. No one's forcing you to do anything, Gill. No one's taking away your ability to get on with your life or go whatever way you need to go. To your friends. To your conference. To your classes. To your house with your brother. I never asked you to stop doing anything. I never once got in the way of you enjoying your life or accomplishing your job."

"Are you saying I'm fucking up your job?"

"No, I'm not saying that. Every decision I make is mine. Like I said, I'm a grown-ass man. I can fall in love with who I want. I can do my job without supervision. I can build my business up on my own merits, all without stopping you from doing what you need. So keep that tragic face to yourself."

She could see red blotches crawling down her arms and across her chest. "You're calling me selfish and unfair."

"No I'm not."

"Just say it already."

"I'm not calling you anything. When have I ever criticized you? When have I ever asked anything of you? When have I ever even inferred or demanded?"

"Well I guess that makes you perfect, huh?" He wasn't going to see her cry, not when she had a façade to maintain.

"Jesus. I didn't say that. Obviously I would never say that.

I'm flighty, and I can't focus like you and Ton. God knows I have dreams way bigger than I can ever hope to achieve."

"You said your business is doing well."

"I'm not talking about my business. I'm talking about my personal life. Our personal lives. That's where I dream too big."

She couldn't take this. Forget everything about her lauded ability to get to the heart of things. Some things had hearts that shouldn't be delved, and hers was one of them. "I'm obviously getting things wrong here. You've made that totally clear. I'll just ....." She stood, because being naked in front of him was not nearly as nerve-wracking, at that moment, as sitting in the sheets beside him. Being too damn close while distress, longing, and anger shadowed his features.

"You're leaving."

She tugged on the clean shirt from her bag, yanked on yoga pants without even worrying about underwear. "I'm—yeah, I'm leaving."

"Right. Of course." He curled away under that grey mottled duvet, so she couldn't even get a glimpse of his expression. Not that she was trying. She just happened to glance his way as she snatched up her things.

"Listen, can we just ... not talk about it for a couple of days?" And something about his voice, how it was hollow like a log that had been eaten away for years by weather and rot and insects and armadillos, rooted her in place.

Finally she nodded, not that he could see her, and made her way to the living room. She called for a Lyft and sat awkwardly on the edge of his sofa while she waited, staring at his walls. They were covered with personal photos. Trips with friends. His parents, waving as they set sail without him. Him and Anton through the years: camping, playing games, hiking, being goofs.

None of him with his family. None of him on a date. And not a single one of her.

CHAPTER TWENTY-EIGHT

THEO AND RACHEL'S family was spending the week before the wedding at the place where it would be held—something like thirty acres of lightly wooded land an hour west of Houston. The hosts were Mary Lynn, Rachel's former neighbor and Hannah's honorary grandma, and the man she, he was told, "ran off with" back when Rachel and Theo first were dating. He was a retired caterer and had all the wedding meal stuff in hand.

Victor went over all these personal details like it made a whit of difference where Goldberg sourced the brisket or how Theo's Austin relatives were pleased with the B&B they'd found. He had a job: take wedding photos. If some of the kids played bocce ball, he took photos. If Mary Lynn and Goldberg cracked up when the flower arch collapsed around them, he took photos. If the bridesmaids kicked off their flip-flops and shed their matching robes on the dock before plunging into the small lake, he took photos.

He couldn't spare the time to zoom in on Gillian. To decipher anything in the expressions caught by his lens. To savor the light playing across her wet shoulders or shrink from the way she ducked underwater when she seemed to glimpse him walking along the bank.

It wasn't his job.

He found Theo with some people from his brewpub, organizing the bar for the next day's reception. Got in some arty shots of steel and glass and hands busy arranging it all. Wandered the rest of the property looking for more of the groups of people joining in to set up the place for the wedding. The tent was up, and most of the chairs set out. Goldberg was back at his pit smoker toying with blocks of aromatic wood. Mary Lynn was rocking a baby he thought at first was Cassandra, but turned out to be a cousin, while Rachel's aunt cradled baby Cass. Everything was busy but relaxed, festive but low-key.

He wasn't going to hunt down Gillian to find out where he should sleep. He could drive back to Houston. Sure, he wouldn't sleep much that way, but it wasn't the end of the world. Or he could search for cheap hotel. The cute B&B was full, but as long as he was around for the usual bridal suite photos, it wouldn't matter where he plopped his head that night. Or if he was covered with bedbug bites in the morning.

The main thing was to be sure that Gillian's friends didn't know he hadn't slept in her room. She didn't want to detract from Rachel's big day by putting their break front and center of the social group. Which was fine by him. He didn't want to answer anyone's questions. He didn't want to deal with people looking at him when they should be looking at Rachel and Theo. He didn't want a pity party. Even if he was pretty much holding one for himself in his heart.

So, fine. He would find a place to spend the night. Didn't matter where. He would do his job. He would go away. Once Theo and Rachel had their prints, he would be out of everyone's lives, no longer a problem, not a burden on Gillian.

In the back of his mind, he imagined Ton saying she'd never called Vic a burden. But Ton's pedantry was not his problem. His only problem was a broken heart. But he was a grown-ass man with a livelihood to attend to. So that's what he did.

He took pictures.

He raised his hand in acknowledgement but didn't join Theo and Dillon and Evan as they huddled together for a toast. He didn't slide into the seat next to Gillian when the others left it vacant for him at dinner. He didn't let on that anything was wrong with them, or that her smile was devastation to his peace of mind. That her eyes were flashing messages he could not afford to transcribe. That he was broken, battered, bruised, and bereft. He did his job. He took pictures. He wasn't part of them. Years from now, when they look back on the images of this day, nobody would notice his absence, and nobody would suspect the gaping hole in his soul.

HER BED HAD BEEN like gravel, which is probably why the gals noticed her gloom. It wasn't like she was moaning about her tense shoulders or hadn't concealed her under-eye circles. She strived to make everything as normal as possible, not even blaming the Velcro-like sheets or clump of straw posing as her pillow. But the gals noticed, somehow.

Maybe it was when Natalie asked if Vic had good shots from the day before. And she shrugged in response. She should have oozed positivity. Odds were it was merited. He'd been moving like a dervish all day. Avoiding her, avoiding conversations, avoiding eye contact. Definitely putting up a front, which she'd only bothered to notice because she had to pretend that there was no issue between them. It was Rachel's day. That was all that mattered.

Later, she could check out the photos and see how forced her smiles were. Later, she would tell them what was happening, or not happening. Or over. For now, she was going to focus on Rachel, on making the day beautiful for her best friend. On infusing every minute with the joy and love she so richly deserved, especially after her first marriage to the snotty slime-sucker. Though she deserved it independent of that weasel.

Rachel was the most true-hearted and giving and supportive person in the world, and honoring her friend was far more important than fussing about her erstwhile relationship.

"Gillian, seriously? Are you even awake?"

"What are you talking about?"

Rachel stopped poking her arm. "I just told y'all that Hannah referred to Depy as 'Other Yia Yia.' And you're not even blinking about it."

A gasp burbled up from her very core. "She did what?"

"I know! Which is why we are all laughing. And you're just sitting there like it doesn't have the potential to turn into a massive gully-washer of a blowup if she calls Depy that in person."

She could just picture it. "Okay, you have to tell Sergei about this. You know, just as a nice little warning."

"Do not tempt me. He can just deal with the fallout when it happens." Rach faked a shudder.

Gill relaxed into maybe the first real smile of the day, imagining Rachel's ex-husband and ex-mother-in-law absorbing the blow that little Hannah called another woman by Depy's grandma name.

"See, now that's the reaction I looked for from you—an evil grin, not staring off into space." Serena accused, "Something is going on."

"Ditto," echoed Rachel and Nat.

"What are you talking about? Everything's wonderful. Just look at Rachel's hair." She drew shapes in the air to imitate the intricate whirls and sweeps of the wedding up-do.

"Yes, obviously, she's radiant. We know this. But you are faking it. So, what gives?" Natalie asked.

Rachel nodded. "Come on. We have at least forty-five minutes of downtime to gossip and giggle in here. And at this point, I think we all have the bridal party prep down to a science. You even painted your face already."

Gillian glanced at herself in the mirror, relieved to be spared teasing about the bad job she'd done applying makeup during the other weddings. She was learning. Reluctantly, but she was learning. Even her eyeliner was on point. "One of these days," she said, "I'm going to show up at work with a full face on, and my department chair will fall over in shock."

As a diversionary tactic, it wasn't her best attempt. Natalie shoved into her personal space and said, "You claim to be lazing off on summer break, but it hasn't stopped you being the quickest to grasp things of all of us. So stop pretending. And stop sidetracking. Tell us what's going on with you and Vic, because one thing I know for certain: something *is* going on."

She sighed and took a look over at Rachel, hoping that at least one of her friends would give her a break on today of all days. Turned out, no.

Rachel studied her nails. "What? I am so full of bridal nerves. I just can't wait to marry Theo and officially make him and Andres part of my family. Tied together all legal and tight like some sort of perfect combination of every one of my dreams that I never quite allowed myself to dream. So, I think what I need today, in the hours before we head up that makeshift aisle, is to be distracted super super lots by the interpersonal lives of my best friends." Her eyes twinkled with smugness.

Serena jumped in. "Totally get you there, friend. Thing is, I'm a newlywed. I'm still in the honeymoon phase in my life, and there's just no interpersonal problems for me to lay at your feet."

Natalie added, "Wish I could help. Unfortunately, I'm in a blissed-out love bubble and can't come up with one single complaint about how life is going now that Evan and I are no longer living in sin."

By rights, she should smack down every one of them. They weren't nearly as funny as they thought they were. Unfortunately, they were all just as full of love and tenderness as ever. And that's what did for her in the end. She tried one more feeble protest. "We don't have to talk about any of this today."

"Oh, but we do," Rachel said. "I needed a distraction or I'm gonna go running over to Theo's room now and drag him down the aisle before everybody else even gets their shoes on."

"Stop it. Like you would deny yourself the pleasure of showing off your happiness in front of your entire family."

Rachel laughed. "Okay, sure. You have a point. Distract me anyway."

If only she knew what to tell them. She knew the facts, of course, such as they were. It was all that horrible emotion underneath them tripping her up. "Okay. So y'all figured out Vic and I aren't together. Good detective work."

"Oh shit," Serena said. "I hoped I was imagining it."

Natalie shook her head. "Evan told me. I didn't want to believe him, but he told me."

Rachel, of course, pulled her into a hug, because no one understood about the comforting power of a loving touch better than Rachel. "What happened?" she asked.

It was as simple as that. Two words, offered with kindness and empathy and an obvious wish to lessen her burdens. And damn her anyway for having already done her eye makeup, because no way was even smudge proof mascara gonna help her out now.

"So, he said he loves me." She stopped. It wasn't much of an explanation, but how much more could she possibly say?

Serena rubbed her shoulders.

Natalie gave her a tissue. "It's okay."

She tried to laugh through her snotty nose. "How is it okay? How can I feel like this? How can we go back to what we were?"

"What was that, exactly?" Natalie asked.

She balled up the tissue and glared. "I don't know. If I knew, I might figure out how to get there. That's the problem."

"So, what's changing, now that he loves you. Or now that you admit that he loves you, I should say, because the fact of it has been obvious for ...." Natalie glanced at the others.

Serena shrugged. "I mean, at least since your wedding."

Natalie laughed. "I was gonna say at least, since he showed up taking pictures at the spa in December."

Rachel snickered. "Me, too."

"Oh my god, shut up, y'all."

Rachel let her smile drop. "Hey, it's not a tragedy to be loved. Trust me on this one."

She squeezed her friend's hand. "Okay, yes, the fact that you're about to walk down the aisle kind of gives away your feelings about love and happy ever after and twelve thousand other situations."

Rach leaned against her. "Hey. Don't think I'm ignorant of what it's like when your friends are overflowing with heart-eyes all over the place. I know our endorphins are a pain in your ass."

Serena said, "Sorry not sorry."

"Of course you're not. You're the one who made us all roll the dice for mates to start with."

Serena shrugged. "Yeah, but that was just to help Natalie over a tough spot. I'm not the witchy one who imbued the whole thing with some sort of predestined success."

Nat snagged another tissue for her. "No point playing the blame game. And also, no point in going on about confirmation bias, which, don't even pretend you're not about to do, Gillian Linette Bellamy."

She pressed her lips together.

Natalie waved a hand to hush the laughter. "So we opened ourselves up to some good sexytimes in our lives. And more power to us. That doesn't mean that Gillian is somehow doomed if she and Vic don't end up together."

"Good thing," Gill said, "given that we aren't going to."

Serena went right for her heart. "Is that for sure? For sure, for sure?"

She yanked out a couple of lipsticks and declared war. "How am I supposed to know? He wants this impossible stars-and-roses life with me. And that's not me—y'all know it's not me. Never has been. He's the one who's known me my whole life. He's the one who's closer to my family than anything, and saw how my parents were, and saw what that did to me and Anton. So much as I love this blissed-out marriage thing of yours, and yours, and yours." She smiled at each of her friends. "And I really do think it's wonderful for you that what y'all want is also what your husbands want. And that y'all can give that to each other. But that doesn't change what I need, and who I am. It doesn't change what I need. So how can he ask it of me?"

Everybody was quiet for a couple of moments. Making vague gestures towards preparing themselves for Rachel's ceremony. She caught them darting glances at each other in the mirror and slammed down her lipstick. "What?"

Serena cleared her throat. "It's nothing, really."

"Bullshit."

"Okay, fine, but you're not gonna like the question."

"As if I haven't figured that out already." She wagged her fingers in a 'bring it on' gesture.

Serena's expression softened. "I get that forever isn't—no, wait. I get that legal ties and a big ceremony aren't things that speak to you. I get that marriage isn't for everyone, and obviously there's no reason it needs to be."

"So?" She didn't even try to hide the petulance in her tone.

"So the question is, does not being interested in marriage also mean that you're not interested in long-term? Does it mean that you and Vic have to separate, that there's no future for you? And if not, what about with anyone else? Is there a reason that you're never going to be in a committed relationship, whatever form that takes for you? Can't you create your own version of happiness, your own terms for what coupledom should look like for you?"

They left her alone after that, which was just as well. Not *alone*, obviously, since they had that whole putting on dresses and fluffing each other's hair thing to be getting on with. When Goldberg delivered a tray of empanadas and guacamole and champagne, Rachel laughed. "It seems more like a beer kind of meal. Not that there's anything wrong with a beer kind of meal."

Serena snorted. "I should hope not. You're marrying Mr. Brew Pub in like half an hour, so it's better you're not starting with a buttload of disdain for him."

Gillian let the champagne tickle her into a laugh. "No, we'll save all our disdain for 'Other Yia Yia' and her butt hurt, blow hard, bronco booger of a son."

"Wow. Sure glad you're not my enemy." Nat blew her a kiss.

"Yeah, keep it that way."

Nat saluted her with her middle finger.

"Elegant. No wonder Evan wants to have your babies."

Serena whipped around. "Wait, what babies? Since when are y'all talking about babies?"

Nat shot her a 'how dare you drop that bomb today?' look that Gillian read perfectly well but refused to be cowed by.

And since, after all, Nat was an amazing friend, and so was Serena, and so was Rachel, they moved on to talking about the scary, enticing, yet somehow alien idea of Natalie having a baby.

"It's just cause Evan is one of a hundred kids," Rachel said. "It's hard to imagine you starting down that path without it turning into some sort of *Eight is Enough* type situation."

"Hello, mother of three. Do you have room to talk here?"

"Okay, fine. My *Brady Bunch* situation and your *Eight is Enough* situation puts us both firmly in the world of sitcoms from last century."

"Anyway, it's not like I said I wanted to have eight kids."

"Just because Evan's family is Evan's family, and Evan's nieces and nephews are Evan's nieces and nephews, and Evan's sisters and brothers are Evan's sisters and brothers and his parents—"

"Yes, yes, yes, you can stop now. I get it. We are perfectly capable of coming up with our own plan for how to build our family without it being a referendum on his or mine either one."

Everyone let Natalie get away with that answer. It seemed like that was the theme of the day, everybody getting away with whatever they needed to get away with. And what Gillian needed to get away with was providing everyone with a solid amount of nonsense to chat about while she mulled over the things they'd said. And the things her heart was inconveniently throwing at her head every minute she didn't actively block it.

Because Natalie was right. She *was* quick to grasp things. And it wasn't at all hard to figure out she'd been about as unfair to Vic as it was possible to be. And running away from him after his pronouncements, instead of staying beside him to talk it out, to figure out if they had more to discuss with each other, or to admit that they had more to discuss with each other because she maybe was a coward, that was a jerk move.

She could concede she was letting fear rule her emotions. But acting like they weren't real didn't prevent her from seeing perfectly well what those other emotions were.

CHAPTER TWENTY-NINE

SHE WAS WATCHING HIM. Maybe it made her a creep. Maybe it made her the worst purveyor of mixed messages to ever mix a message, but Gillian couldn't deny that she was watching Vic as he went through all of the motions of his job. Everyone he talked to, it was with an easy smile. Time after time, he coaxed their joy in the day to shine in their faces as he captured the wedding guests. Even the kids were perfect for him, posing as directed. Rachel had told her that, between the photo session before Cassandra's birth and the kayaking party, Andres and Hannah were completely comfortable with Vic.

"They act like he's part of the family," she said, and she wasn't even trying to be pointed about it. Just her normal maternal self. So it wasn't like she could be grumpy about the observation.

She couldn't figure out—what she told herself she shouldn't even try to figure out—was how real was his smile? Was he just acting the part of geniality, or did he really feel as relaxed in this company as he seemed? Was his growing closeness with her friends' husbands surviving the tension between her and him? Or had she destroyed that, too, when she called him out for the way he clung to her family and not to her, specifically?

She tried to stop staring at his sunshine face. Tried to stop being aware of the way he circulated in the room. But she wasn't having much luck.

Serena plopped down beside her. "What did you think of the ceremony?"

Gill's face softened. "It was perfect, wasn't it?"

"Even when Goldberg's ducks waddled down the aisle eating all the flowers Hannah had scattered?"

She laughed. "That was the most perfect part. That, and when they all huddled together for a family hug after the 'I do's."

"Yeah, that kind of got to me, too."

"You really did turn into a sucker for love, didn't you, Serena?"

"Fuck, yeah. Plus, what's fun about marriage is all the sex, and how he makes me breakfast. I never knew a morning person could also be such a late night guy."

"Oh my god, stop bragging about all your orgasms."

"I can't help it. They rock."

"Brat."

"So ...." Serena said, pasting on innocence as she toyed with salad.

"So what?"

"So, made any life-altering decisions in the past couple hours?"

"You're the worst."

"But you love me."

"Clearly."

"And you're going to spill, right?"

She rubbed her forehead. "What do you want me to say?"

"Nothing special. Just, like, 'hey, it turns out that when you hired Vic to take your wedding photos, it was the best day of my life.' " Serena reached over and snagged all the bell peppers Gillian had shoved to one side of her plate. Not because Gillian disliked them, but because Serena adored them and she knew handing them over was inevitable.

"Thanks."

"Anytime."

"And about the rest?"

Gillian wanted to look around for an escape from the conversation, but doing so would mean catching Vic's eye. She knew because, even without actively watching him, she could tell he'd drawn closer to the head table. "It's not like I've had a ton of time to think about it."

"And yet." Serena's sarcasm lost her a couple of pepper slices.

Plus, crunching into the vegetable allowed her to delay her response for a precious few seconds.

"Come on. You can't deny that you're the one with the quick-thinking brain. I know you have thoughts."

"Well, you're Ms. Intuitive over here. I bet you can read my thoughts without me having to say them."

Serena snorted. "Do you think if you don't say them, they're not true? Do you think you can just pretend you have the healthiest emotional life of anybody in the Houston-Galveston-Fort Bend Metroplex?"

"Ha ha." Gillian pretended she wasn't grateful for the lifeline of her friend's banter while she mulled over what to say to Vic.

"Just asking. Anyway, you get your reprieve. Here comes the man himself, and it's almost time for your maid of honor speech."

Gillian growled just loud enough for Serena to hear her, and plastered on an expression she hoped suggested that Serena was laughing at something besides her personal distress. She, Natalie, and Serena raised their glasses together in a toast while Vic lined up a shot of them.

Once he lowered the lens, she caught and held his eye. Serena was right. She didn't have to articulate a thing to understand what she needed to do next. And she could only hope that the glint in his eye meant he understood that she would seek him out later for a further conversation.

And for the apology she owed him.

THERE WAS something in her expression. He wasn't imagining it. He was a skilled and sought after portrait photographer who understood how to read faces. So he knew when there was something in her expression. Thanks to that whole skilled professional thing. He didn't have more than a few minutes to seek her out during Theo and Rachel's wedding reception. And thanks to the fact that she had goddamn hurt him by running away when he confessed his love, he wasn't exactly making a point of putting himself in her way.

He had to hightail it from Brenham to Houston after the reception so he could organize himself. He was meeting clients at the airport first thing Sunday to head out for a week-long destination gig.

In the dark of the next Saturday night, he pulled into his garage and dropped his head to the steering wheel. Felt like the first time he'd stopped moving in days—months, even. Not that staying busy on Islamorada had been a problem. Earlier in the summer, he'd thought maybe he could get Gillian to join him in Florida. He'd ended up relishing the chance to be somewhere where nothing reminded him of her. Now he had to head inside his house, past the table where she'd sat and pretended there was nothing odd about how she never come up with schemes to see him.

He could go in and sleep on his old bedroom, under the quilt his parents had made to commemorate their twenty-fifth anniversary. But all those uneven hand stitches and fabrics commemorating their devotion to each other didn't feel like they'd be any more comforting than laying in the bed where she'd pretended they had nothing to discuss. Pretended sex could smooth over any of his disquiet.

Still, it was better than going to Ton's and sleeping there, knowing she was just on the other side of the wall.

He went for the next best thing. Texted his best friend: you around?

Ton: Yeah, for another few days. Why?

Vic: Just got back into town Thought you might want to bring me a pizza

He didn't have to wait long for Anton's reply. One thing about the Bellamys: they were quick-witted and and on the ball.

Ton: Spinach and chicken or bacon and peppers?

He relaxed enough to blow the air out of his tight chest. This was good. This was what he needed.

Vic: bacon

Ton: Bacon. Got it. See you in 47 minutes.

He responded with the twins emoji, which said everything he needed Anton to know.

CHAPTER THIRTY

SHE WAS twelve thousand miles of nerves in a body built for fifty. Her brother had given her the puzzled look he turned on their parents and other people so much more than on her. To him, it was simple: she had a plan, everything was in place, and either it would work or not.

But no amount of preparation took her toes off the knife's edge. Anton sent her in his truck. The garage door code for Vic's house was programmed into his console. It gave her maybe one and a half minutes of grace before Vic would know that she was the one showing up with a pizza, instead of Anton.

She balanced her package on top of the pizza, but wasn't brave enough to carry her overnight bag in from the car. The kitchen was empty. And the way her breath caught somewhere between her sternum and her throat was an unnecessary reminder about how much she wanted to see Vic, but didn't want to live with the unknowns of this conversation.

"Ton?" he asked.

She cleared her throat. He was walking her way. "It's not Anton."

He stopped in the kitchen threshold. "Gill."

She tried for a confident smile. "I brought pizza. Bacon as requested."

He crossed his arms and didn't reply.

"Sorry for the ambush." She couldn't tell if he was staring at her because it had been too long since they were together, and he wanted to soak up every inch of her. Or if he was trying to figure out what he'd ever seen in her in the first place. She was crossing her fingers for the first one.

She set the boxes on the table and smoothed her hands down her thighs. "If it's okay, can we talk?"

He took two steps towards the table and the rubber bands stretching between them eased just enough for her to drop her shoulders.

"I'll go, obviously, if you want me to. But I really needed to see you. To apologize. And, Vic, I'm so sorry. It's—let me ... I'm stumbling over myself. Sorry, I want to talk to you. And I want to explain myself. And I want to tell you so much." Her voice hitched, and she trailed off.

He looked at the pizza. And at her, and out the window, and back at her. "Do you need a beer?"

She wasn't sure he could even see her nod, he turned so fast towards the fridge. She let a blip of optimism spur her to grab a couple of plates and napkins.

He looked at the other box she'd carried in, but didn't ask anything as she moved it onto an empty chair and sat across from him. "Thanks."

He pursed his lips and nodded. "Thanks for the pizza."

"Anton says he'll make it up to you for the trickery. Says he'll show you how to get through that boss level without losing stamina."

His grunt was unamused, but he hadn't thrown her out. So she took a deep breath and stuck with the plan.

"Remember when we were camping and Cisco said that about us all being tied by the hips?"

He nodded.

Her throat was dry but she wasn't allowing herself to be refreshed by the beer just yet. "So, I realized, I've known you for so long as this ... extension of Anton. The Tony twins, ride or die, all that stuff. And here's the part where I say never mind what my parents or anyone else thinks: Anton is not a problem I need to solve. I've known that for ages. The only thing is, at one point, he kinda was my problem. Not in an unwelcome way. I've never thought of my brother as a burden, and never could. He's just part of my life, and it was important to me to find ways to help him bridge between his world and," she waved towards the window, "everything out there. I've been doing that since before you knew him."

Vic nodded and slid the pizza box an inch her way.

She flopped a slice onto her plate. "I never thought I was jealous of your role in his life. Never thought you were something else I had to fix or solve or mitigate or observe cautiously —none of that. But I always took for granted that you and I were the most important things to Anton. And since I knew what my role in his life was, I realize now I took it for granted that your role in his life was essential to you in the same way."

"I love Anton."

She's smiled. "Of course you do. No one's ever doubted that for a microsecond, any more than they doubt it about me. But I'm trying to say that I guess I always assumed you were on Team Anton in a way that could be ... therapeutic, too. I go around anticipating dangers all the time, worrying about people being cruel, worried about him not understanding some social situation. Laying whatever groundwork I can to make his life easier. Getting to know his teachers, his peers, his boyfriends. And I just guessed—from the way you always got him involved in friendships and activities and even mischief sometimes—that you were actively laying groundwork like I was. Your own version of it."

"It's called friendship, Gillian."

She picked a piece of bacon off the pizza. "I know, I figured that out. Way, way too late. But I figured it out."

He didn't jump in to reassure her that he got all she was trying to say. Fair enough, since she wasn't exactly following the plan to explain herself.

"I'm not on track. Everyone always says I'm on track all the time, but I'm not on track right now, and I'm sorry about that. Thing is, you and Anton, you're best friends. And I love that. He's always been there for you, and I love that you've always been there for him. And I'm trying to learn to be the right kind of there for you, too, and the right kind of there for him. For him, I need to be a sister and a friend, but not a protector, not a guardian. Not always looking for something that's going to hurt him so I can ward it off before it does." She pleated her napkin. "This whole time, even before I thought about you and me as an option, us spending more time together and getting to know you as a friend. As the man you are now and not the kid I knew long ago, or the fuck boy—"

"Fuck boy?"

"Yes."

"Thanks for that."

She leaned in. "But, see, that's what I've done. I got into this relationship with you without ever dropping the 'he's my brother's friend' thing, the same way I've never dropped the 'I have to protect my brother' thing. I'm sitting here, over and over and over again for months, being surprised that you're all grown up now. That you're a man in your own right. But I'm the one who was being immature and stuck in my childhood. I'm the one who didn't take you as you are now and understand that I was falling in love with Victor Anthony. I wasn't falling in love with Anton's best friend, who I needed to approach like the most important thing was to protect my brother from the fallout. If there was going to be fallout. Or to make room for Anton, if you and I were going to be together. That wasn't fair to you. Wasn't even fair to me. It was short sighted and unwise and it clouded me over and here I am, in love with Victor Anthony. And I don't even know how to deal with it."

"Hang on." Finally, his eyes flicked up to hers. "In love?"

She wanted to gaze at him without the scrim of tears blocking her sight, but it was just impossible. "Desperately, yeah. Desperately in love with you, Vic. I mean it—with *you*. Not with some version of you I decided was the truth, before I ever met you on neutral ground. Not with a guy I can spend my life with because it will make my brother more secure. Maybe I fucked us up too much."

She bit her lip. Swallowed. Kept going. "I'm pretty sure I did fuck it up way too much. But you snuck up on me, Victor. With your kindness and your insight and your bright side of everything and your goddamn sexy humor and your heart." She broke off and buried her face in her napkin. "You snuck up on me, and now I'm just ...." She shrugged. Wished he would talk. Knew he wouldn't until she'd said her piece, because he was Vic. And for all his physical restlessness, he called up infinite amounts of patience to let emotions enter the space when necessary.

"I'm grateful, is what I'm trying to say. Grateful that you said you loved me, and grateful you made room for me in your life. Without you, how would I have ever accessed this forever kind of feeling I have now? I wasn't ever looking for that. I'm not champagne and roses, I'm not fancy parties and grand gestures. I'm just a cynical professor who gets too caught up in her inner monologue and too distracted to get on with things without setting a hundred alarms to remind me to stop working."

"I love your hundred alarms."

See, she could be wrong. There he was interrupting her, and she wasn't even done pleading her case with all the ways he was perfect for her. "You can't like my hundred alarms, they're overkill. I should just learn to make dinner at a proper time like a proper adult." The goddamn napkin was not soothing on her snotty nose.

"Why?"

"What?"

"Why do you have to learn to stop work and make dinner without an alarm reminding you? You found a system that works for you. You're not hurting anybody with it. It's not something you have to change, Gillian."

She scoffed. "Tell my mother that."

He scoffed right back. "I will not. It's something she should have figured out already. But you can't think I want to discuss your parents right now."

Damn, the way he got her. It would be unnerving if she wasn't so thrilled every time his simple statements proved that she wasn't less-than in his eyes. So she scrubbed her face again and went back to her plan, which seemed like it might truly be working.

"Victor. I love you. Maybe I waited too long, and if I did, I get it. Because you're not the kid I knew. And you're not some-body whose heart I can take for granted just because you're my brother's best friend and that somehow turns it into a walk in the park for you to be with me. To put up with everything I ask of you. I know I've taken you for granted. And I know that's unfair. And I know I ambushed you today. You say the word and I'll leave. I'll stop talking about all this and give you space to eat your pizza alone."

She laughed a little. He did not. Damn but his eyes were soft.

She felt her throat and her stomach and her palms and her knees in every beat of her pulse. "Before I go, though, I just want to promise you that I mean it. And that it's not casual, it's not fleeting. It's not going away anytime soon. Or, ever. So, when you're ready to talk to me—*if* you want to talk to me—you know where I am. I'll be waiting, and I won't make it bad for you. I won't be awkward. I'll stay out of Anton's unless I'm sure you're not there."

Every molecule of air had rushed out of her body. A shame, since it would have been nice if her brain could have had the oxygen to process the moment. She thought she'd said it all. She thought she'd completed the plan. But it felt like such hollow work to stand and leave. She tossed her napkin into his trash can, patted her pocket for her keys.

CHAPTER THIRTY-ONE

SHE HAD to get out of his house. The whole silent place was a rebuke to all of her dreams.

"Gilly-Bean."

She spun so fast she was dizzy. It wasn't just the tease of her nickname. It was the tenderness in his voice. He was standing, hands shoved into his pockets and brow line furrowing to the top of his scalp. It wasn't a look that should have forced her into a smile.

"What's in the box?"

Was it a trick question? "Bacon and spinach pizza."

He didn't step towards her; she'd have been able to tell if he was stepping towards her. But still he seemed closer. "Not that box." He nodded towards the chair.

She'd have laughed if any of that breath of hers had returned yet. She wasn't as good at plans as she'd thought. "It's a gift for you. If you want it."

His brow cleared and his cheek creased in a half smile. "Will I want it?"

She cleared her throat. "Kind of depends on whether you want me."

"Will it sway me one way or the other?" God, how could he

tease her? He was too sweet and sunny for this torture. But here they were.

"I don't know. Just open it already and then you can decide."

"Seems like you might want to open it for me."

Oh, could he *not* enjoy her tension? It was unfair.

He crossed his arms and leaned back against the kitchen counter. "You tricked your way into my house. Seems like you had a reason, and the pizza wasn't it."

She would throw things at him if he weren't so generous and patient and sexy all the rest of the time. "Fine," she bit out and snatched up the box. "It's just a token. It's not like these are as good as yours. I never would say that."

She fumbled open the flaps and set to battling the plasticky padding around the frame. He stilled her hand and took it from her.

"It's a picture?" He slid it from the box and deftly managed the wrapping.

"It's four pictures. Well, three." She stated the obvious. He could see the collage frame for himself. "Like I said, they're not professional like yours. But at least the frame looked like a match to what you have in there. Those ones with your family and Anton and everything." She shushed, because what on earth was she even going to say when the pictures each spoke their own thousand words? Let him respond to them however he would.

Except it turned out she couldn't let things speak for themselves. It was the problem with being a linguist. He could use pictures, but she had to use words. "I asked our friends for help. The gals, the husbands. Everybody went through their cameras and phones and stuff until they found all these different options. I didn't even imagine there were so many pictures of you and me. Anton picked the final ones. I came up with a shortlist and made him pick which were the best."

He gazed up at her. "Gillian."

"I mean, it's just a gesture. I'm not a Valentine's Day and

elegant dates and all that kind of person, like I said. I'm just me, but ...." She looked back at the frame.

The first picture was her and Anton gazing at each other on New Year's Eve, confetti in the air proving it was just past midnight.

The second, a surprise contribution from Jorge, caught them laughing and leaning into each other while dancing the Hora around Natalie and Evan.

The third had mortified her when she'd first seen it. It was one Evan had taken during Rachel and Theo's reception. Vic was raising his camera to the group of them at the head table. His lens blocked the view of everyone else, but she was perfectly in focus, and completely focused on him. Watching him with her heart in her eyes.

"Gillian," he said again, a near-whisper.

"I am not a big fancy party person," she said, maybe for the dozenth time since she arrived. "I've never imagined marriage for myself, or even anything that might get serious. But I think I've been cheating myself that way. I think if I'd allowed myself to break out of thinking about everything in traditional roles, and just thought about my dreams sooner, I'd have realized those dreams can include being committed. Can include being so damn in love with someone like you."

He was so close to her now, the frame resting face up on the table between them. He touched the empty slot. He was a picture-worth-a-thousand-words man, so she understood the question without him having to voice it.

"I was thinking that someday, we might move in together. Or something. And then we could have, like, a housewarming party. And maybe when we do that, we could count that as some sort of, you know, big moment for you and me. A commitment to be together. To love each other. If that sounds okay to you, once you believe that I really do love you for you and not because any wrong thinking of mine. And once you can trust me to be there when you need me. So then if we do something like that. God.

This sounds so ridiculous now. I'm sorry, but it was the plan, and I'm going to tell you the plan. So the plan is that we have this party, and someone takes a picture of us, and we can add it in here, and it could be the next step on our journey together. If you want to take a journey with me."

She stepped back. Because the plan was to give him space and time. The plan was to say her piece, give him the photos, and wait. However long it took.

She filled her lungs again. "Okay. So, if you want to call me. Or just show up. Or tell me to come here." Damn, she was crying. "I'll fit it all into your schedule. Whatever you need. I want to make that room for you."

And maybe her plan worked. Something in his soul-soft eyes clued her in. Maybe she could staunch her tears and squelch her fears and believe how Anton told her that her plan was enough. That all she had to do was let him know that she was gone for him and they'd work it out just fine. She hadn't even had the sisterly spite to goad him about him and Cisco. But he hadn't been a bratty brother and warned Vic what she was up to.

She risked a longer look at her beloved. His eyes were still tracing the framed photos, shoulders relaxed and wide enough to brace herself against while she waited for his verdict. Because even though the plan was to walk away and let her pictures ask their thousands of questions while he decided how to answer them, she'd done enough research to know that sometimes the plan had to change on the fly. She inched towards those solid shoulders. Felt the warmth he radiated reflecting back on her face, as she relaxed into stillness, finally ready to drop her defenses and accept, unguarded, whatever he had to say.

CHAPTER THIRTY-TWO

"IT WON'T WORK."

She flinched when he said it, and he decided he'd earned that tiny bit of pettiness towards her. Just this once. Because keeping her in suspense was inflicting harm, and Victor wasn't in the business of inflicting harm on anyone, much less somebody he loved.

"I can't wait for us to get around to hiring movers and planning a party to take this last picture. We should do it now."

She gushed out a breath, her eyes crinkling into happiness.

"There is something you got wrong, though."

She studied the frame. "I ... okay. Tell me."

"When you said I wasn't laying groundwork to help Anton, with all those activities of ours." He rubbed at his nape. "I mean, I wasn't, I don't think. You were right about that. But it's the joined at the hip thing."

"What about it?"

"You told me once I just wanted to be a part of the Bellamy family. Like I wouldn't have chased you around weddings all year if you weren't Anton's sister."

She flushed. "That was rude of me. I just—"

"No, it's fine. I know why you said it. But where you got it wrong is that Anton already was my family. Has been forever. I didn't drag him from pillar to post trying to find a way to ease him into social situations or make him feel valued for who he is. If any of that happened, it was a side effect of what I was really doing."

Gillian studied him with her keen eyes, probably making all the connections he had gone too long without himself naming. She swallowed hard. "It was a good side effect, though. It gave me a lot of security, especially when I was heading off to college."

"Well, that's good. Even if it wasn't necessary because of that whole 'you're not your brother's keeper' thing."

She wiped under her eyes some after her short laugh. "Touché. So what were you really doing?"

"Dragging him from pillar to post? I was pretty much using him like I use my camera now. Hiding behind him while I scoped out the situation. Looking for ways for him to care about theatre or whatever gave me a way in for myself. Ton is my security blanket. My best friend and my brother and—" He grinned. "I used to say my most important person. Don't tell him I'm calling him one of my top two people now."

Gillian grinned right back. "I hope I'm the other one."

"Hell, yeah."

"Thank fuck for that." She glowed up at him, gorgeous and intent and, he was beginning to believe, his.

He tapped the empty photo space. "I think we should head to my bed, have hot makeup sex, and take a selfie."

Her head thudded against his shoulder when she let out a pained laugh. "You drive a hard bargain."

"Well, we can have the hot makeup sex here, if you want. But you might get pizza on your ass."

She flung herself into his arms and he was so ready for her. Ready to hold her and support her and keep her beside him for whatever came next. And to kiss her. God, he was ready to kiss her. Two weeks without kissing Gillian Bellamy was a crime he intend to never commit again.

Her hands on his butt gave her leverage as she pulled her bodies together. He scraped his fingers into her rich, soft hair and ensured there was no distance between their lips as they moved down the hall to his room.

After pouncing on her, and pounding into her, and practicing just enough restraint to ensure she was writhing and bucking and coming all over him, he exploded. "Gillian. Fuck. Gill. I love you."

Her answering cries were echoes and reverberations and promises he could put all his faith in. Sated, she slid into the space beside him. Rested her cheek on his still-heaving chest. He kissed her crown. "I love you."

"You mentioned that." Her voice was dream-light and relaxed.

"I know, but I told you once when I was hurt and angry. And I told you again in the middle of passioned fucking. I wanted to tell you now, while I am deliberate and content. Because you deserve to hear it when you can treat it as an everyday statement."

She drew her fingers along the line of hair on his chest. "It sounds like you've been spending too much time with a linguistics professor, getting all into the syntax and context of your words."

"Maybe I have. Imagine what I'll sound like after another decade or two of your influence."

"Ugh, I'm such a bore. Just tell me to hush when I go on too much about my work."

"Nah. I like your brain. I love watching how it works. It's a real turn-on." He nestled her more securely under the crook of his arm, then squeezed her ass. "Just so you know, I love your body too. Don't want you to think I'm only after you for how smart you are."

The shiver that went through her sparked bright flashes in his chest. "How do you always say things that melt away my moodiness?" she asked.

"Part of the service, ma'am."

"Yeah? What service is that?"

"The being your boyfriend service. Or your partner, if we can go all official here."

She pressed up enough to take a good look at him. "So you meant it, about the selfie?"

At least some of the devilry that flashed through his mind must have appeared on his face, because she turned red and ducked her head. "Behave."

He absolutely would not. "Don't scold me. You're not in charge of me. Partners remember that. No more big sister stuff."

"I remember. That's the main thing I wanted to get across with this big plan of mine."

Probably he shouldn't bask in such self-satisfaction at the idea of her putting that big brain to use to convince him to do what he had decided months ago to do anyway. But bask he did, and decided to allow it for himself.

"I love you," she blurted.

He laughed. "Yeah, I got that, thanks."

"I'm saying it in contentment. Copying your idea."

The littlest statements from her made him glow. Good thing she was planning to commit herself to him, because he was such a goner for her.

Lucky he'd left his phone charging by his bed while he waited for—he'd thought—Anton to arrive. Easy to grab it while keeping her plastered to his side, thumb up the camera app, then tilt down to nuzzle her while he snapped photos. Even if she did squirm and mock-protest and yank the covers higher on their bodies.

"Come on, I'm only framing our faces."

"You'd better be."

His whole body could float into the stratosphere, he was so beyond happy. "Take a look."

She snuggled even closer as he swiped through the shots. A few were blurred to hell, and others caught skewed mouths or closed eyes. But the first two, and one from the middle were good. And then: "Wow."

She wet her lips. "So wow."

It wasn't high art. He'd have to balance the exposure and fill in where the pillowcase had pulled back and exposed an off-white strip of the pillow underneath. But the focus was on their eyes, all crinkled in delight. At being together, at being a couple, at being in love. It was him, and her, being entirely a *them*.

Still, he offered. "We can take more, if you want."

"Nope. No way. I demand we use this one."

"Demand, huh?"

"Hey, I'm the one who thought up the brilliant photo frame idea. The artistic director, if you will. So my opinion holds a bunch of weight here."

Never mind the stratosphere; he was in whole other galaxies of goodness. "I bow to your aesthetic demands."

"I bow to your good judgment."

He caught her in a kiss that soon turned into yet more exploration of their bodies, and their hearts. He was one damn lucky man, and it would be a daily thrill to reinforce to Gillian how glad he was that they'd taken a chance on each other. And won.

EPILOGUE

A COUPLE of months before Vic even moved in, she and Anton sorted out their attics and spare rooms to store all of their camping gear between their houses and the garage. Then they knocked down the old shed at the back of the garden. With a prefab and help from one of Anton's contractor friends, they set up a new studio for Vic, complete with a brick path from the driveway to the new space.

He'd known it was coming, but gave into their demands that he stay out of it until it was complete. His only job had been to let Ton take a bunch of measurements from his house and to point him to some blogs about studio spaces. It was true that his best friend was a genius, so he tried to not spoil the surprise by sharing too many of his last minute ideas. Anton would figure it out.

Meanwhile, he and Gillian kept growing closer until, for both of them, cohabitating was more of an urgent need that a fantasy wish. He told her he'd manifested them living together by saying from the beginning that they'd fall in love and commit to each other. She told him he was full of literal nonsense and should go chill out at Serena's instead of pestering her while she was trying to finish up the semester's grading.

Box by box, trip by trip, he shifted his possessions to the her place. Finally his stuff was either moved or sold off. The walls in both halves of the duplex shifted to display his photos. Ton absorbed a lot of equipment into his gaming system. Vic and Gillian slept under his decidedly more comfortable blankets. They filled out gaps in the Bellamy kitchens with assortments of his cutlery and serving bowls. All in all, by the time Vic's buyers had their final walkthrough, the entire duplex felt more like his own home than the house he'd grown up in ever had.

But, of course, wherever the Bellamys were always had that distinction.

He went to his old place one last time to check all the cupboards and closets. And to retrieve the item he'd hidden in his garage. He didn't think Gillian suspected, but he kept it wrapped in a padding blanket in the rear of his vehicle just in case.

Everyone showed up for their New Year's Eve party. Serena and Dillon. Natalie and Evan—neither drinking in deference to Natalie's pregnancy. Rachel and Theo, without a single kid in tow thanks to visitation schedules and a babysitter. Jorge, along with his husband Bubba. Others, too: his new neighbors, a group from Gill's college, Theo's cousin and Dillon's and Evan's coworkers and their partners. And, of course, Anton with Cisco, still strong despite the drags of their demanding travel schedules.

He let Gill and Ton blindfold him when they led him to the new studio. The evening light had faded, leaving everyone to trail him by the glow of solar lanterns and twinkle lights. It turned out his trust in them didn't quash his nerves. He wanted to like it. Wanted his reaction to live up to their excitement. Even Anton was playing it up to the onlookers, which Vic knew he didn't like to do in any kind of crowd.

Like she got him—like she was passing on permission for him to have an honest reaction—Gillian squeezed his hand. "Ready?"

He leaned his shoulder into hers and nodded. Anton

thumped his other shoulder twice before swiping off his face mask. They'd draped the door in a hodgepodge of recycled wrapping paper, taped together in a hilarious mess with the occasional gift tag or bow still stuck to it. The whole ridiculous thing made him whoosh out all his nervous tension.

And then he entered. And it was ... perfect. They'd covered the prefab's large north-facing window with a diffusing shade, and mounted his backdrop rig on the wall perpendicular to it. The floors were reclaimed hardwood, sturdy and with a matte gleam that would look stunning photographed. His desk and client chairs made for a welcoming entrance, and the layout was spacious enough for accessibility needs while giving him plenty of options to arrange his reflectors and lighting stands.

"We modified the bathroom to be a half-bath and changing area," Ton said.

"And look," Gill pulled him to the filing cabinet next to his desk. They'd installed a mini-fridge and coffee maker beside the cabinet.

"Damn." He'd known how to make words before, but the skill was lost to him now.

"Is it good?" Her face wasn't as uncertain as her words, but he clocked how intently Gillian studied him.

Before he could get out an answer, Jorge wriggled past the crowd to get inside. He let out a low whistle. "Damn."

So true. "That's what I said."

"I had an elaborate fantasy once about having a place like this."

Bubba grunted behind him, but Jorge shot him a 'you fulfill all my fantasies' look that set Bubba to smiling wickedly.

He was pretty sure he sent that same look Gillian's way all the time.

Including right there in front of all their friends—and Anton, who was the rock of their family.

"This is amazing, Gill. Ton. Thank you."

"Thanks for taking the chance on living here."

Ton nodded in agreement with his sister.

Fuck if he wasn't gonna cry any second.

"Come on then, take a picture or something. Show us how the magic happens," Evan said, bouncing a little in the general air of excitement.

He felt like his grin was flushing through every pore in his body. "Give me just a sec." He planted a kiss on Gill's cheek, then Anton's, and wriggled his way out of the crowded doorway.

Passing Dillon, he asked him to be sure all the gals were in the studio. Then he jogged out to his trunk to get the box he'd hidden for so long, detoured through his and Gillian's place to pick up his Canon, and met the gang back in the studio.

His studio. His own workspace, customized for his needs by the two people he most loved. He was a goddamn lucky man. And he was going to make a speech about it.

"A year ago tonight, I kissed Gillian Bellamy for the first time in years."

She flushed a fascinating red and buried her head in Rachel's shoulder while everyone cheered and whistled.

"Right? It was a great idea. And over the next several months, I got to see Gill not just at the home of my best friend, but at the weddings of her best friends. It was amazing to witness all these couples pledging their love for each other, and to know each set of those vows was also bringing someone else more tightly into Gillian's life. But after all those 'I do's of theirs, Gillian told me in no uncertain terms, 'I don't.'"

The gals and their husbands all laughed, which set the rest of the onlookers at ease enough to chuckle along. Gillian glared at him, and then at Jorge, who'd taken Vic's camera and was capturing the scene he was making.

"To be fair to her, she told me she loved me, but wasn't interested in marriage. Which was fine, because all I'm interested in —feels like all I've ever been interested in—is loving her right back."

He didn't know if Rachel gave her a push or if she moved on

her own, but Gillian floated over to fit her arm around his waist. He leaned down for a not-brief kiss while everyone made 'aww' noises at them.

"That night, she proved her commitment to me by speaking my language: she gave me a collage of pictures of us from all those weddings, which summed up so well how we fit together. I filled the last picture in that frame with a selfie of us after we'd confessed our not-so-secret love to each other."

Evan knew how to wolf whistle, it turned out.

"Yeah, yeah. Anyway. Anton helped her with that grand gesture, which just goes to prove what a great friend he is. And now, he helped me with this one of mine, so you all know he's a super brother, too. In case this brilliant studio he helped build me wasn't already proof. He told me where you'd gotten that frame, Gillian, so I could get this one to match." He handed over the box, which she took with slightly shaky hands. "Also he let me practice my speech about a dozen times, since like I said, it's really pictures that help me express myself."

She'd opened the box. He'd removed the wrap from it so she could just slide it out no problem. The three photos on display were of the four friends posed in happiness at Serena's, Natalie's, and Rachel's weddings.

There was, of course, an empty display slot. Her gaze traced it, then moved up and caught his.

He had to clear his throat to finish his big speech. "Another not-so-secret feeling of mine is that you and Anton are my true family. Always have been. But living with you, loving you, has given me so much more of a family than I'd ever imagined. Each one of those weddings brought those people..." he smiled over at Serena, Rachel, and Nat, who were holding hands and watching them intently, "you wonderful women and your pretty great husbands, into my life. And so, I wanted to commemorate that bond, of how we have become family to each other, with a fourth photo for this frame. I want to capture this night when

I'm committing to you, Gillian, in front of all our people. Will you let me break in my amazing studio by posing with your gals?"

He glanced at Ton, who gave him a nod to assure him he'd said all the things. Swallowed and looked down at Gill. She licked her lips and her eyes were doing that glinting thing he adored.

"This is perfect. Thanks." She held it up for the crowd to admire. "Book him now for all your occasions, friends. My beloved is a hell of a good photographer."

He lowered his voice so just she could hear him. Or so he could pretend that to himself, because he didn't want to blow all his credibility by showing his nerves. "You do like it?"

She pressed closer to him, squeezed his side. "You've laid all these words on me and robbed me of speech. Except to say: I love you."

"I love you."

"Okay, break it up," Serena called, "we were promised a photo session." The laughs rippled out from his chest and through the studio and out into the people still in the yard. He was looking forward to giving them all tours. Soon.

Jorge handed back the camera and went to help Anton switch on the lights. Vic set a stool in front of the backdrop and guided Gillian onto it, and didn't have to utter a word to encourage the other women to crowd in around her.

Only problem was, he had to take a moment to wipe his eyes clear before he could take the pics. Seeing Gill there, in this new space she'd made for him, surrounded by the friends who meant so much to her, and now to them both ....

He blinked away his tears and focused on the camera, solid and familiar in his hands. "Okay, ready? On three." The friends leaned together. He raised the lens, and everything in him radiated with the joy, and clarity, of knowing he was home.

THANK YOU!

Gillian was in no hurry for me to bring her to a Happy Ever After conclusion, but I delighted in helping Vic change her mind as he captured all the beautiful moments of Serena, Natalie, and Rachel walking down their aisles. I'm a lucky author to have enjoyed so much time with the **Roll of the Dice** gals!

Ratings and reviews truly help me grow as an author, and I appreciate all of your feedback. Please take a moment to review me! Goodreads - Bookstore

Not done with me yet? Read on!

My 'also by' page has links to the rest of the **Roll of the Dice** series, as well as my other books. My 'about the author' page has links to my newsletter, website, and social buttons. I'd love to connect with you!

Happy Reading,

Melanie

ACKNOWLEDGMENTS

Robert is my best friend and wisest copyeditor and pretty patient about letting me ramble on and on and on and on as I brainstorm. Plus, he kept me in bird feeders as we strove for ways to endure 2020. Making it through a pandemic together is a sure sign I wasn't quite as impulsive as our right-out-of-grad-school, moving from other countries, four-month long engagement might suggest!

I'm always grateful to the communities at Contemporary Romance RWA and the Inclusive Romance Project, especially to my frequent writing sprint pals. I'm excited about the progressive direction of romancelandia, and glad to be a part of it as it becomes a better part of the world.

I set the publication of this book for the week Joe Biden and Kamala Harris took their oaths of office in the US. I wanted to be able to celebrate the release of my tenth book in a world less shadowed by authoritarianism and overt bigotry. There's so much work still to be done, and so many people who aren't safe. I am incredibly privileged to be able to write happy everyone after stories for a living, and I thank everyone working to create happy everyone after realities for the world.

ABOUT THE AUTHOR

Melanie Greene lives in a little cottage in a giant city, with her husband and kids and cat and dog and all the people inhabiting her imagination.

For more info, visit her at www.melaniegreene.com, where you can sign up for her newsletter to access new releases and bonus content. Also visit her at Facebook.com/MelGreeneBooks and Twitter.com/Daki_MelGreene.

ALSO BY MELANIE GREENE

EXCERPT FROM ROLL OF A LIFETIME

RACHEL PACED the convenience store aisles, paying little attention to the packaged foods, the stacked cases of beer, the three donuts left in the bakery case. All she noticed was time ticking away at the rate of two strides per second. Four seconds per aisle, turn, four seconds more. With each step, something on the sole of her left shoe clung, lightly, to the linoleum. It didn't alter her pace.

She would stick to her pace until her ex pulled into the parking lot with their daughter.

He was late. Still no text. Still no call.

Three minutes, fine. He'd been three minutes late with handoff before. Five. Eight. Thirteen.

Eighteen.

She checked the map app. No signs of slow traffic anywhere near. No accidents or high water, despite the rain darkening the sky. She gripped her phone as she paced, hedging against thunder drowning out the sound of a call.

If he was driving, navigating slick roads and maybe Hannah getting cranky as dinnertime approached, she didn't want him answering a call. Fumbling for his phone instead of keeping his hands on the wheel.

Chip aisle. She scanned for snack options. Wouldn't be the first time he'd failed to account for normal toddler pickiness and returned her hungry.

Candy.

Automotive accessories.

Energy drinks.

She pulled up next to the sunglasses display, where she had a partial view of the parking lot between signs for the Texas Lotto and a flyer for the local high school's year-end musical. The phone rang four times before someone at the host stand picked up. "Thanks for calling Elixir, how can I help?"

"Is Sergei there?" He wasn't supposed to work during his custody weekends, especially when his mom was out of town. Didn't stop him from dragging her daughter to the brewpub.

She got a cheerful "Hold on," and curled the phone to her clavicle to avoid listening to the recorded upbeat spiel about new summer beers and Thursday Trivia Nights. It took deliberate effort to avoid memorizing it. She turned towards the magazines. But all the glossy covers under fluorescent lights made her queasy. She could practically smell the competing perfume samples in the women's mags, and as for the men's stuff. No. She didn't need to be yelled at by a bunch of cars and boobs.

The voice returned. "Sorry! Can't locate him for the moment. Can I leave a message?"

She managed politeness as she declined. Not this guy's fault his boss's voice snaked through her mind. *Pestering my employees now, Rachel? Try a little self-control for once, can't you? Stop acting like every half-formed thought that makes it into your head constitutes a national emergency.*

She flinched, and then glanced at the man behind the counter to smile an apology for making a spectacle. He shrugged back at her. Setting an oat bar and juice bottle on the counter, she searched for more time-consuming distractions. Even if he'd just left work, they'd arrive within ten minutes. She would do herself a favor and not spend them counting the seconds.

Back to the sunglasses rack and the partial view. Not that seeing the parking lot magicked Sergei's car into it. At least the rain had slowed to a mist. Rachel sighed and uncrossed her arms, the better to rotate the display of eyewear. She alternated trying the white-framed Jackie O style and the smoky aviators as if choosing was the weightiest decision she'd faced in the thousand or so days of her daughter's life. Maybe the glittery purple pair with star-shaped lenses? Hannah would adore them, but she couldn't picture cycling to the daycare wearing them. They'd probably bash the underside of her helmet.

Just past the slim strip of mirror, she caught sight of the dark, sporty SUV that still twisted her stomach five months after he steered its shiny rims off the lot. Sergei was still paying back child support from his between-jobs periods, but his silhouette at the wheel was as nonchalant and above it all as always.

She was at the vehicle before the door chimes had quieted. He was bent into the back to retrieve their daughter. Fine. No matter how it galled her, getting loud directly to his smug face still gave her the shakes afterwards. So she ranted at his narrow ass. "We have a schedule. *She* has a schedule. Did you ignore it the whole time you had her, or only this afternoon? How is she supposed to—who the hell are you?"

––––––––––––––

THEO CUT off his one-sided conversation with the toddler and, hitching the overnight bag higher on his shoulder, turned to locate the owner of the royally pissed voice.

"Mama," said Hannah, lunging at the woman so eagerly she for once loosed her grip on her blue elephant. Theo gathered her to him, trapping the stuffed animal between them, and earned a whap from the plastic brachiosaurus in her other hand as thanks.

Wincing, he asked, "Rachel Groff?" He held off on passing back the girl, just in case. It wasn't that he doubted it—her daughter's reaction was enough to go by, even without Sergei's inadequate sketch of a description. Blonde. Shortish. Dressed in 'mom clothes,' whatever Sergei meant by that. He'd given Theo a blank look when he asked for a picture, as if the idea of having a shot of Rachel in his phone was absurd. Theo had a few of his ex, and not because he was hung up on Annalisa. She texted him pics of their son, and sometimes she was in them. If he'd sent Andres off with some random guy in search of her, he'd at least be able to show the random guy what Annalisa looked like.

Not that he was random. Which he needed to explain to Rachel before she blew another fuse. "I'm Theo."

"Good for you. Is that supposed to explain why you have Hannah? And yes, I'm Rachel. Give me my daughter."

She didn't wait for his compliance, but reached over and helped herself to the child. He held up the bag. "Want me to stick this in your car for you?"

"Where is Sergei? And who are you? Why do you have my child? Did you even belt her in right?" She was peering into the back seat as if the configuration of car seat straps would prove his negligence.

"Of course I did. Look, I have a little boy; I know how to work car seats. And Sergei's the one who put her in the seat. And I checked it before we left."

She was still exuding non-verbal displeasure.

"Sergei works for me," he said again. Or maybe for the first time. The woman had him off-kilter. "I'm Theo. Theo Melis? Did Sergei not tell you I'd be bringing her to you?"

She made it clear the question didn't need answering. Not that he hadn't gleaned the truth. Seemed Sergei's hand wave when he'd checked about this plan was dismissal, not acknowledgment. All so the man didn't have to reschedule a meal with a vendor he shouldn't have planned for a custodial Sunday.

"Let me see your driver's license." Command, not request.

He set the overnight bag on the hood and reached for his wallet. "Sure. You gonna run a screen on me so you know I'm a safe driver for next time?"

She motioned for him to hold his license still while she snapped a photo of it. Maybe later he'd ask himself why he was following this woman's grumpy dictates.

"You're never driving her again."

The declaration was firm and her jaw was jutting and he was too polite to get into a fight about it all. He slipped his wallet back into his back pocket. "Sorry, sure. Whatever you say."

"Are you mocking me?"

"Would I mock your mama, little Hannah gal?" He pulled a long face, eyebrows up and chin tucked down.

Rachel huffed and swiveled so she was between him and her daughter. "She doesn't like strange men."

Hannah leaned around Rachel and pointed at Theo, smiling like he was the latest craze in animated unicorns. He wiggled his ears, not because he thought the toddler would notice, but because it would irritate her mom.

Hannah giggled. Rachel glowered. Theo laughed.

"I'm sorry. You're very stern, and I'm cowed, I promise. Although it's hard to take you seriously when you're wearing all those glasses."

Her free hand covered her forehead and he tried to hold back a snort at her growl. She paused a moment, then whipped the purple star lenses off her face and the other two pairs from the top of her head. Her eyes were bluer than her daughter's, and at the moment twice as large. He wasn't sure if she was enraged or embarrassed, but either way she was enthralling.

Theo held out his hand. "Can I help you with those?"

"It's fine. I don't need help." She glanced back at the store, lifting the fistful of eyewear. "We're heading inside anyway. Let's go, okay, Hannah banana?"

He let her walk away, but called out before she was stuck juggling glasses and child to open the convenience store door. "Rachel?"

Her pivot towards him was as slow and rigid as she could manage, he guessed, given her burdens. "Theo, was it?"

He hefted the overnight bag. "Can I carry this in for you?"

Those blue eyes narrowed. She hitched Hannah more firmly on her hip. He debated, too late, the wisdom of baiting her. Her one-word answer was a slingshot of civility. "Please."

She turned back towards the store, and the face he made as he approached them was probably responsible for Hannah's renewed giggles.

———

HER NOW-WET SOLES squeaked and stuck on the linoleum as she carried Hannah to the checkout. *Squee, squee-pop, squee, squee-pop.* The stranger who'd propelled her daughter in a two-ton vehicle stalked after them. She ignored him in favor of burying her nose in toddler curls. Seemed Sergei had managed to parent long enough to give her a bath over the weekend.

The star-rim glasses got caught in her own hair as she shifted Hannah to the other hip. If the stalker man—Theo—hadn't been so late, she wouldn't have even looked at the sunglasses. After wearing merchandise straight out of the store on top of abandoning Hannah's snack on the counter, she'd rather buy all three pairs than fumble excuses for herself. So there went forty not-so-spare dollars, and Sergei's buddy was still lurking when she turned to leave.

"Excuse us." Because Aunt Johnston's lessons in politeness bubbled up when she couldn't let loose in front of her child.

"The bag?" He hefted it like it was a game-show prize.

It was her favorite one, with room for every possible contingency. She wouldn't pack it for Hannah's overnights with her father, except Sergei refused to keep clothes and diapers for his daughter on hand. He claimed it was because she grew too fast for him to keep track of her sizes. Rachel's friend Gillian claimed it was because he would never take on the emotional labor of parenting if there was the tiniest of loopholes available.

Gill was the most cynical person she knew. And in this case, certain to be right.

Rachel worked on stuffing the juice and sunglasses in her purse. She gave herself a half-second to close her eyes, then reached for the bag. "Thank you."

He sidestepped so the door was clear. "Anytime."

Big surprise, he followed them into the parking lot, and to her car. Not to Sergei's, a whole four spaces away, but hers. Just stood there watching as she jiggled the key in the lock—a pattern she could do in her sleep, but wasn't so easy when her arms were laden with daughter and bags and Effie, the most vital stuffed elephant in Texas, threatening to slip past her elbow and straight into an oily rain puddle.

She felt a tug, and swiveled her neck to see Effie being danced behind her shoulder, which meant Hannah leaned into her instead of away, which made balancing the straps on her other shoulder easier. Which meant she got the door unlocked and could sling purse and diaper bag towards the passenger seat.

He used the wrong voice to make Effie trumpet. Way too low and not nasal enough. Pathetic, for someone who claimed to be a parent.

Aunt Johnston's voice niggled at her, which Rachel preferred to Sergei's insidious grasp on her subconscious. "Thank you."

Something about the way he bit the inside of his cheek as he handed Hannah her elephant told her he wasn't fooled by her polite words. She slid inside the back seat to buckle in her daughter, as content as it was possible to be about how very clear her dismissal had been. When she emerged to take the driver's seat, he was gone.

www.ingramcontent.com/pod-product-compliance
Lightning Source LLC
Chambersburg PA
CBHW011455170626
46814CB00009B/3063

* 9 7 8 1 9 4 1 9 6 7 2 2 5 *